Down-Under Shorts

Stories to read while they're fumigating your pants

GERRY BURKE

Down-Under Shorts
Stories to read while they're fumigating your pants

iUniverse books may be ordered through booksellers or by contacting:

iUniverse
1663 Liberty Drive
Bloomington, IN 47403
www.iuniverse.com
844-349-9409

ISBN: 978-1-4502-0948-9 (sc)
ISBN: 978-1-4502-0949-6 (e)

Print information available on the last page.

iUniverse rev. date: 12/11/2020

EXPLANATORY NOTES

Flemington, Caulfield, Rosehill, Morphettville, Doomben
Deniliquin and Donald are venues for thoroughbred horse racing.
Phar Lap was Australia's greatest racehorse.

The Dapto dogs are for people who are barking mad.

Sandringham, Prahran, Heidelberg, Niddrie and Dandenong are
Melbourne suburbs. Tatura and Somerville are country hamlets.
Bondi is a Sydney suburb.

Strine is a slang language peculiar to peculiar Australians.

Fair suck of the sav is an expression of bewilderment that is rarely
used by vegetarians.

ACKNOWLEDGEMENTS

Editing Services: Kylie Moreland

The intelligence community in England, Australia and America for their extraordinary tolerance in the wake of uninformed hyperbole and improbable case histories. As is usual in exposés of this nature, names have been changed to protect the innocent. I even tried to change my name but the publisher wouldn't hear of it.

INTRODUCTION

A former Australian prime minister was once observed in the lobby of his overseas hotel, embarrassingly underdressed. He was wearing his underpants and enquiring about the whereabouts of his trousers. I know how he must have felt. In the kind of sleazy hotel that I frequent, you send your slacks out for maintenance and hope that they don't end up on a street person. It is quite a gamble.

You will be relieved to know that my short stories and social commentary are more about gambling than dry cleaning. My first book *From Beer to Paternity* painted a picture of a long-suffering bachelor, continually spurned by beautiful women, obstinate racehorses and inconsiderate money-lenders. That's about it, really. Everything else that you read will be totally fictitious or measured by at least six degrees of separation.

The following articles and opinion pieces are an extension of my first volume and will help you better understand me and where I am coming from (Australia).

We are all gamblers in our own way and like to take chances, whether it is in the field of politics, entertainment, sport or travel. These are the topics that I mostly write about and they call me PEST. Fortunately, I am quite thick-skinned.

Gerry Burke

Table of Contents

-1-

OTHER GENERATIONS

Chinatown

The young and the restless

There has always been a generation gap. When one thinks about people of another time and place, you sometimes feel hopelessly impotent. The next generation has you completely frustrated and don't you wish that you knew more about those who have gone before?

I live in awe of the Chinese people and especially admire their tolerance in relation to the elderly. Confucius and I are old friends and this friendship has been cemented over many years. A round table at one of his celebrated establishments is always de rigueur when you have experienced a winning day at the races.

The story on young people is a different kettle of fish. Actually, some of it is about fish so it is a slippery slope to climb. Nevertheless, the youth of today should never be ignored and it is possible that some of them may appreciate my commentary. I say that it is possible knowing full well that it is highly improbable.

CHINATOWN

The octogenarian was seated in his usual chair, silently surveying the daily rituals as they unfolded before his ever alert eyes. There would be no betrayal of any emotion but he was feeling smug and satisfied with the world and all it had to offer. In the main part of the restaurant, his children and grandchildren worked the room as befits any servile servant of the Ling dynasty. The old man could be well pleased. His children were fertile and productive and hard workers all. Their eating establishment had long received the accolades that it deserved and was the recipient of ten Good Food Awards. His take-out service sold more egg rolls than the combined efforts of five other Chinatown restaurants. But he was a long way from home and nothing would give him more pleasure than to return there before he passed on.

Sixty-five years earlier, the adolescent Li Ling Ho left his village in the northern province of Shandong and travelled to the big city. He managed to secure some menial work with the British Legation but his timing was all askew. There was immense dissatisfaction with all the foreign colonials and for fifty five days from June to August of that year, Beijing was under siege. The insurrection was called the short Boxer Rebellion. Or was it the Boxer Short Rebellion? Never mind. It was a precarious time. Houses were boarded up and the streets were awash with blood. I don't know what the tourists were thinking. With most of the restaurants closed, it would have been difficult to get a good Lemon Chicken.

As it turned out, there was one man in town who would have been able to acquire this for you. His name was Larry Ling and the shy kid from the sticks had quickly morphed into the most talented procurer that the Empire had ever seen — not that he confined his services for the benefit of Her Majesty alone. He was a gopher for the French and Germans and also kept the Japanese supplied with sushi. The young man may have even saved the day for the forces behind the fortifications. Those who defended the compound only had one heavy firing unit. The cannon was nicknamed the *International Gun* because the barrel was British, the carriage was Italian and the shells were Russian. Do I need tell you who put the whole thing together for a very reasonable commission? From all sides, mind you.

Although he was an ambitious man, he was not impatient. Ling maintained his ties with the British for over four years and in that time was promoted from the laundry to the kitchen. In his quarters you might find all manner of collectibles, much of it being illicit contraband. For a Chinaman, he had quite a reasonable singing voice and every now and then he would be invited to perform at the Governor's monthly tea dance. His most prized possession was a recording of the famous American entertainer George M. Cohan. The record went platinum in 1904.

When Li, now known as Larry, was ready to depart the kitchen of Her Majesty's service, he could boil, braise and burn with the best of them. If he ever got to America, which was his dream, he had decided that he would name his signature dish after the city that had given him his first real break. It mattered little that all the Americans that he had met around Peking were absolute wood ducks. Over at the Rising Sun legation, the head honcho had his eye on Ling. He liked what he was doing with raw fish and the young fellow had already established some kind of reputation with his sushi deliveries. In the aftermath of yet another international incident, the Japanese were in the act of annexing Korea and there were opportunities for young people with drive and enthusiasm. They were also looking for people who could design golf courses. However, that's another story for another time.

The food business!

Larry loved the hustle and bustle of Beijing/Peking but he was less excited about Korea's frenetic capital city. It may have been his new-found maturity but he believed the heart of Seoul was nowhere near its main arteries but in the peaceful tranquility of its outer reaches. So, that's where he set up shop. He hired an attractive girl from the neighborhood for front of house and reached out to the local residents, who were yet to experience the delights of food that was good to go. In fact, eating at home was not only a long-term tradition but it would take a super salesman to convince them that anyone could cook better than their wife or mother.

Of course, they had under-estimated the man from Shandong. He was not only a super salesman but a whiz in the kitchen. Naturally, he had to adapt. The British Embassy would have no truck with the likes of barbecued rat or sun-dried frog legs but Larry made them both half-price specials on his Monday and Thursday menu. There was also the double advantage of reducing the amount of vermin around the kitchen.

The Korean adventure was a huge success and he probably had no reason to leave, except that the girl at the front of house was only fourteen years of age and she was pregnant. Oops! Needless to say, Larry hit the road running with many incensed relatives in hot pursuit. He managed to make the port city of Incheon, where he stowed away on a tramp steamer bound for who knows where. The man must have been blessed with bad luck because two days out he was discovered and put to work in the galley. The provisions were meager and there was little variety but in no time at all, he had won over the crew with his brilliant imagination and superb culinary skills. So, they threw the previous cook overboard and wouldn't let him off the ship.

In 1937, Larry had re-surfaced in New Guinea and established a business in one of the main towns, as many Chinese had. He was still a long way from America but he was about to have his credentials endorsed by people who really counted. Two Yanks, Fred and Amelia, had arrived at his restaurant for a late night meal, prior to their departure from Lae the next day. Evidently, they had their own plane and were involved in some kind of round-the-world record attempt. Larry recommended his renowned egg roll, pork entrée plus number sixty-nine and eighty-five with fried rice. Naturally, they also opted for the banana fritters and green tea.

Mr Noonan and Ms Earhart were so excited by the quality of the food that they invited Mr Ling to join them and they chatted for quite some time. Amelia explained that her local Chinese restaurant in LA was so inadequate. She wrote him a reference and urged him to come to America as quickly as possible. Ling enquired whether there was any room on the aircraft the next day but he was informed that the extra weight would impact on the fuel usage. As we all know, the airplane disappeared somewhere over the Pacific Ocean and Larry Ling lost what could have been his most important mentor. To this day, that framed reference hangs proudly above the old man's seat in the Ling Ho restaurant.

The optimistic oriental finally managed to get stateside but it wasn't until ten years later and rather than Los Angeles, he set up shop in San Francisco. This was postwar America and the whole country was hungry for good food. Some years later, flower power would intoxicate this city with a passionate concoction of love and benevolent goodwill but at this time it was a dangerous place to live.

The Mob just happened to be crazy about Chinese food and caused all kinds of interruptions to daily service but you just lived through it (hopefully). My father was passing through the city around this time and wanted to be part of the Chinatown experience. After being seated, he enquired as to what had happened to the three tables over in the corner of the room. The wallpaper had been stripped back and a number of lackeys were mopping the floor feverishly. It transpired that during a birthday party for a popular Mafia hit man, one of the mobsters had taken exception to the message on his fortune cookie and sprayed the corner of the room with his machine gun. He took out three clergymen, who were enjoying a social prelude to their appearance at an ecumenical conference. Management, in their inscrutable way, maintained operations as if nothing had happened.

I should mention that the framed testimonial from Amelia Earhart was not the only artwork that adorned the walls of the Ling Ho. All manner of celebrity dropped by to chew the fat with Larry and a happy-snap was part of the deal. The compliant ones then had access to that portion of the menu that was unavailable to the peasants and other people who didn't move in exalted circles. What they didn't know was to their advantage. The food was exactly the same but given a different name and an inflated price. Larry did weddings, wakes and bar mitzvahs for the rich and famous but not for everyone. He missed out on the Joe Di Maggio/Marilyn Monroe wedding breakfast because the film star was on a diet. As a tribute to Clint Eastwood, he served up the Dirty Harry Dou Foo Tong, which was a bean curd soup. Clint always used to say: *I don't care what it's been. What is it now?*

As Ling's children grew to an age where they could be useful (serve in his restaurant), he realized that they were fast becoming more American than Chinese — an observation that was shared by many of his contemporaries. A journalist of the time, Audrey Wong, explained that New Year's Day comes twice a year to San Francisco. For one generation, the year starts on January 1. The traditionalists look to January 31 when they acknowledge the year of the pig, dog, rat or some other farm yard idol. She claimed that the westernized version of New Year's Eve is usually one day of debauchery. Chinese New Year carries a heavier meaning for many people. Wow!

Renowned Confucian historian Arthur F. Wright declares that the father should be a wise ruler and his dutiful children are properly submissive subjects who know their place, their role and their obligations to others. Give over. When are these people going to wake up in the real world?

I don't know whether Larry cared much about Wright or Wong but he did know that he had a serious issue on his hands. Perhaps he could handle his sons and daughters but the grandchildren were out of the park. One of them turned up for work with purple hair and a ring through her nose. There was even a rumor that there was even more metal work, yet to be uncovered.

It was comforting to know that the patriarch became more understanding in his old age. It probably had something to do with his fading eyesight and poor hearing. See no evil. Hear no evil. The amount of the daily takings was still relayed to him at the end of the evening but he no longer checked them on his abacus. There was no need — one of his grandchildren was a digital whiz-kid and another was chief accountant for a notorious loan shark. He was not sure that this was a good thing.

If you visit San Francisco, you will still find Li Ling Ho in his favorite chair but no, he will never see the northern province of Shandong, again. He will still have his memories and what can you say about the legacy that is a large family? If I could borrow from that great Gucci advertising line: *He will be remembered long after his prices are forgotten.*

The man and his mush!

THE YOUNG AND THE RESTLESS

There is something about young people that completely mystifies me. It is their ability to basically ignore rational thought and considered analysis in order to arrive at a definitive position and then communicate same in their very own truncated version of the vernacular. The lad who usually serves up my morning espresso has often given me the impression that he is a Prime Minister in waiting. His expressed views on the environment are pertinent, if not over-simplified. When asked whether he had considered a career in politics he replied: *Hey man - the Minister for the Antarctic! Totally Tubular.*

I think that everyone agrees that this would be a real cool job and the fact that such a position does not exist is totally irrelevant. I believe that his enthusiasm would hold him in good stead, no matter what portfolio he was allocated. Anything to get his finger out of my coffee.

Members of my profession spend a lot of time in cafes, bars and bistros. With table service what it is, you get plenty of time to observe and contemplate. I have heard that Leo Tolstoy wrote War and Peace between courses at a Moscow restaurant. One could only hope that their Strawberry Blintz was worth waiting for. I have to admit that most of my research has been done in bars rather than eating establishments. I have liberated many worms from their tequila bottles and embraced quite a few Margaritas. It is what we do in order to get the creative juices flowing.

Prior to the television and computer age, there were very few opportunities for young people to express their ideas or opinions. You either opted for a soap box on Hyde Park corner or you marched from your university campus to the Trades Hall, where you could connect with someone who was an expert in social malfeasance. Today, you can blog your heart out or project your magical talents on Facebook, Twitter or reality television. In my era, we would never admit to being a twit.

On reflection, I was pretty forthright in my youth, as were others of my generation. Jake immediately comes to mind. When he didn't get his own way, he always produced an embarrassing hissy fit. Once, he decided to jump out the window, which was quite a commitment as we worked on the tenth floor. The guy was out on that ledge for almost two hours, while the rest of the staff debated whether to try and discourage him. Eventually, the vote tipped in his favor but in retrospect, this was a poor decision. Today, the fellow actually is a government minister and when push comes to shove, most of his constituents were happy with either.

I have strong opinions concerning the promotion of the young and inexperienced and you will read these thoughts later. Unfortunately, Jake fitted into this category. His personal life was a mess and his timing was always out of whack. At one stage, his missus, the maid and the mortgage were all overdue. The voters didn't know this when they elected him into the Lower House and they expected him to be the life of the party. Even the big city's Chinese mayor dropped by to offer his congratulations. He said: *Jake's erection will mean big things for the community.* Of course, everybody knew what he meant.

His financial worries started about the time that they promoted him to the Cabinet, as the new Minister for Gaming. There were also other debilitating overheads. He had moved the maid into a granny flat behind the Lonesome Cowboy bordello, one of his imprudent real estate ventures; although he claimed that his investment portfolio was sympathetic to the party's electoral platform. They were supporting working families. He was supporting working girls.

Enough of Jake. Let me tell you about Jill. This is not someone that I know but a perfect example of appropriate assertiveness by today's youth when confronted by a pompous git. I am sorry to say that the pompous git was a friend of mine and I do admit that I am acquainted with a number of individuals who are all very pretentious people, especially where food is concerned. For some reason, their palate is the envy of masticators from Macadamia to Old Cape Cod. If you know a few people like this, you will readily recognize the clinical description that is usually attributed to those who are burdened by this heavenly affliction: wankers.

We were just south of Capricorn and the previous evening we had tied one on at the Boat Club, to farewell the departing crew members. This didn't leave us much from our budget so we dined al fresco but modestly. Our dinner arrived in a cardboard box accompanied by sachets of pepper, salt, mustard, ketchup, brown sauce, black sauce and mayonnaise. The chippery was doing a line on barramundi and French-fries for $8.50 and I was reasonably impressed. Not so my companion. He wanted to know whether the delicacy was wild, farmed, salt water or fresh.

Now, I don't know about you but there have been a few times in my life when I have crumbled under the resolute stare of a strong woman who doesn't take crap from anyone. The lass behind the counter was all of eighteen years of age and a bit overweight — probably due to the fact that she was about seven months pregnant. The customer dockets were mounting up so she may also have been a little overwrought. I braced myself for the retort that I knew was coming: *How the **** do I know?*

When you come to the eastern seaboard, it is customary to open the window of your holiday apartment, take a deep breath and exclaim: *Ahhhh, fish.* But she was a local and given her situation, I can understand that she would have little interest in the pre-natal history of Queensland's pre-eminent taste-treat. When order number twenty four arrived, it was beyond recognition, having been battered, braised, bruised and belted into a scaloppini of very flat proportions. It was the kind of offering that they slip under the door when you have an infectious disease. I think that Jill did her generation proud. You just can't be bamboozled by bullies from a bygone era. Fish is fish and if she maintains her stance, she will remain queen of the boardwalk and the fisherman's friend for many years to come.

The intrepid traveler!

Once you get me going on fish dinners, the memories keep flooding back. I have experienced a perfect paella in Palencia and a brilliant bouillabaisse in Biarritz. I was in France to brush up on my vocabulary, which had bewildered many on my previous visits. I remember being accosted by a rather chic lady in the street who seemed to confirm that I was handsome, charming and gracious. It later transpired that she wanted to know on which side of the road she should catch Le Bus. Sacré bleu! Another one gets away and it's all down to that elementary conversation course at Alliance Français. You've got to do it folks.

You don't expect to find a Quicksilver surf carnival at Biarritz as one considers the place a bit refined for that kind of thing but the young studs were all there in their Billabong board shorts and the babes were bouncing about as babes do. I've been to this particular French paradise on about five occasions and marveled at all it has to offer. The Quicksilver Classic is Europe's major surf carnival and is always held on La Grande Plage. Jake and Jill will both be there because Strine is spoken for the period of the contest. The young and the restless! They will be on the beach. I will have my head in a chaff bag.

On the road, I often dine alone but not by choice. Certainly, the kind of Gallic dinner guest that I would prefer is someone who is well-read, presentable and kind to animals. Someone like Brigitte Bardot! The alternative is not pretty. You just have to drum your fingers on the table and wait for your meal. I had ordered La Poulet de Bicyclette and I was wondering how it was going to arrive.

```
ROYAL MAIL
  HOTEL
MEEKATHARRA W.A.
PHONE * 089 981-1148


REG 14-10-02 18:00
 C01        0103   63328
              1


BISTRO DINN OPEN
                $ 15.50
POOFTER DRINK   $ 3.00
CANS SUPER      $ 4.00
TAXABLE         $ 20.45
GST             $ 2.05
CASH
             $ 22.50
```

The poofter drink was a Bacardi Breezer.

When I was fourteen years of age, all I ever wanted to do was open a brasserie. The confusion of youth! From my observations, running a restaurant looked like hard work as the table turnover was constant and some of the patrons were a bit cranky but the staff was never judgmental. I still shudder when I think of my last meal in Western Australia. OK, it was a mining town and *Priscilla, Queen of the Desert* had recently passed through but to put that homosexual outrage on my bill was indeed outrageous.

The dowager at the corner table was a bit like me — a sad sight. Dripping in jewels and elegantly attired, she was fussed over by the waiter, who knew a good tipper when he saw one. I suppose there are grandchildren somewhere and the occasional companion who remembers Douglas Fairbanks when he was a junior. Nevertheless, I had the feeling that her next meal would be served by someone in a white coat.

I hate to digress at such an interesting part of my narrative but if there are some young people who are actually reading this tribute to senility, I think a sobering lecture is appropriate. The true test of love and friendship cements itself over time. Will you need me when I'm sixty-four? The Beatles wrote many enduring melodies but none more relevant than this one. One can only conclude that they all appreciated their grandparents. Today, the adolescent majority can sometimes be intolerant of dementia, incontinence and Doris Day double albums. Nevertheless, it's all ahead of you and be prepared for the worst. I know of no aged care facility that will pipe Animal Cannibal or Snoop Dogg into their entertainment area.

Meanwhile, somewhere in France, the kids are self-destructing in a Maison Miserable and having a great time. At breakfast, I am conversing with my grapefruit while they are engaged in post-coital bliss and contemplating the size of the day's waves. If there is no sunshine or surf, the options are reduced but this is still a beach worth watching. In fact, you can observe the whole world walking by for the price of a café noir. If you want to see your whole life go by, you can venture over to a nearby dirt patch and observe the local geriatrics playing their beloved Pétanque. This is lawn bowls without the lawn.

Soon it is time to pack your baguettes and move on but not before one last visit to our see our future leaders at play. I don't think that there would be any recruits for the Antarctic Department, here but climate change may well be an issue. I was impressed by the ability of penniless students to exist comfortably in one of the most expensive towns in France. If they know how to overcome adversity, they will have the required steel to be a strong leader. Nevertheless, it will be strange to have a Prime Minister with a degree in surfing.

Good to go!

I'm not sure when I first became restless. It was a long time ago. As a young man, confined to the limitations of home and family, those first seeds of wanderlust start to germinate and when you tire of parental control, educational boredom and sexual frustration, you just hit the road. I must have been a man before my time because today backpackers rule the world, not to mention the economy. Most would claim consuming curiosity as their motivating urge to geographically penetrate the other side of the world but in truth many just want to get their rocks off away from the suffocating supervision of their peers, parents and parole officers.

Young people take chances and that is why so many of them leave our shores to seek fame and fortune overseas. The success of our people in Hollywood is an obvious example and haven't they done well: Mel, Nicole, Russ and Naomi? Even if any one of them had been born in this country, I don't think we could love them any more.

Admittedly, they are all getting on a bit and I suspect that this year's Oscar will go to some pubescent nymphet who cut her teeth as a drama queen on the OC or some other teenage television soapie. But you can't discount the Oscars and I know that I'll be there and sweating on a ticket to the red carpet. Don't you just crave the opportunity to be within cooee of a superior being? *It's the Pitts* says one breathless commentator as Brad and Angelina step forward, closely followed by Mr and Mrs Steven Spielberg and Mel Gibson. Oh dear! I hope he wasn't driving Miss Daisy.

Unfortunately, you can't buy a ticket to the Oscar presentation. Entrance is by invitation and we're only talking about A List people. They made an exception when King Kong was nominated but this year, there are no gorillas in the list. It's a bit unfair, really. Innocuous poppets like Lindsay Lohan and Paris Hilton always get a gig and I don't believe that either of these young ladies has an extended attention

span. They just cannot remain out of the limelight for long. You may not have noticed but seconds after they depart from the front stalls, each is replaced by a formally attired professional seat warmer. This is the world we now live in. It's all about bums on seats.

Because I am a bit of father figure to my young readership, I cannot complete this communiqué without commentary on something which is close to their hearts — music. To be perfectly honest, I have to admit to being tone deaf, a situation which has existed since the release of Metallica's first album. I know that this will disappoint many of you but it will require me to abstain from any kind of critique that might otherwise alienate my own fans. Nevertheless, some cautionary advice is not out of place, here.

Even in my day, rock'n roll could be a bit perilous for the average teen. Given that the performers often dabbled in recreational substances not usually approved by the food and drug agencies, concert venues were sometimes dangerous places to be; especially if you had front row seats. A few bad prawns from the pre-concert supper and Chuck Berry was bound to live up to his name. Jerry Lee Lewis was universally known as "Killer." So, if you are approached by a rock star, never exchange fluids with them, don't hitch a ride on their personal jet and try not to play Russian Roulette with their security staff.

Other than that, I cannot think of anything that might give your dear mom an early coronary, should she be acquainted with your current lifestyle. Nevertheless, to be on the safe side, it's probably best that you keep that information to yourself.

-2-

POLITICS

Leader of the pack

Is that your country calling

What can you say about politics and politicians? Not a lot. We all want a better world and we put our faith in our elected representatives to help achieve this aim. This confidence is totally misplaced but where would the media be without them? We can't totally exist on a diet of philandering sport stars and the errant adventures of minor celebrities.

Please don't expect any insightful political analysis in the following pages. These are my rag-tag thoughts, musings and occasional rants, harvested over a number of years and peppered with hokey memorabilia from the family archives. Some of my friends were a little put out that I didn't mention them in my first publication and I am happy to oblige, here.

It is always best to get the boring bits over early, don't you think?

LEADER OF THE PACK

Governance can be so disappointing because people let you down. You have great expectations. A beacon of light in a sea of mediocrity! Then your political savior founders inexplicably because of just one rash, imprudent, ill-advised and brainless act. I have never voted for anyone who has subsequently been accused of having it off with a passing stranger on their parliamentary desk. Others have. They reported that they didn't think that he had it in him or her, as the case may be. My guys have gone down the traditional path: pork barreling, misappropriation of funds, assault and battery and expense account fraud. You have to hand it to that chap in England who diverted funds in order to maintain his castle moat. You don't get much of that in Australia.

Every few months I like to break bread with some of my long-standing friends and acquaintances. They are not political animals but they should be. The Goose, The Gorilla, The Rat, The Ox and The Smarmy Red Ferret were real mongrels in their heyday but they have matured with such charm. They are always totally composed and I am now very impressed with most of their considered judgments, especially when they haven't been drinking. I was just saying the other day that any one of them would make a fine leader and it wouldn't matter which party.

Who can you be sure about, these days? Although it was given to me in jest, I still possess that badge which declares that you shouldn't trust anyone under forty. My friends are all the better for their extensive life experience and this is important because it can be a bit of a jungle out there. The young upstart may have drive and all the enthusiasm of a tiger but how many times has he or she been around the block? Some politicians will be as dreary as a wet weekend in Wigan and others will regard their ascension as a divine right. John F. Kennedy was once asked what he wanted for his birthday and he said Connecticut, Rhode Island or Massachusetts. He was later to become the Senator for Massachusetts.

When JFK came along, he was one of a kind. Then Robert arrived and they were two of a kind. Both of them could have been film stars and this observation has merit because politics can sometimes be very theatrical. Abraham Lincoln was shot in a theater and Ronald Reagan was shot in Hollywood. Quite often!

Unfortunately, style rather than substance seems to be a priority amongst voters and spin doctors are an unwelcome addition to the party machine and their election armory. They don't make the trains run on time but they do camouflage inefficiency and incompetence. None of my pals would ever think of employing such a person unless it was me and I applaud that type of judgment. In fact, the more I think about it, The Goose would be just right in the big chair.

We have already had a goose as Premier but this would be different — especially if he could get The Gorilla in as his second banana. There would be no factional issues because they are on the same wave length and there would be no rats in the ranks. Well, actually, there would be one but he is a bit down in confidence at the moment. Ever since Jimmy Cagney mouthed those immortal words: *You dirty rat*, the vermin population have experienced bad press. Notwithstanding their glorious efforts in the trenches at Tobruk.

One still expects them to be fast up a drainpipe and their ability to desert a sinking ship is an ideal prerequisite for a career in politics. Just because your leader happens to be on the nose, there is no reason why you can't come up smelling like roses. What price ambition if it can't include crafty re-positioning and devious destabilization?

O.K.! You don't like my suggestions. Even before I've got to The Ox and The Smarmy Red Ferret. Alright then! Let's go with the candidate who is dashing, eloquent, charismatic, witty and disarmingly attractive but I do warn you; some of the aforementioned affectations can conceal snobbery, delusions of grandeur, a lack of intellect and similar baggage that is best left to the likes of superior beings in the medical profession and retired statesmen. I realize that there will be a bit of a safety net with advisors and experts on the payroll but this doesn't put my mind at ease. After all, I used to be a consultant myself, once.

What! You didn't vote for The Gorilla.

The sexual situation described in my opening paragraph is only hearsay but nevertheless, widely reported. The politician involved is youngish and disarmingly attractive so doesn't that prove my point? If I was still an advisor, my conservative side would shine through. People who indulge in that kind of activity just have to learn to lock the door.

Your elected representative!

One of my favorite television shows was the British comedy *Yes Minister* and I can distinctly remember the Minister for Sport as a habitual smoker with a terrifying cough. It delighted me when, in a classic example of political expediency, they made him Minister for Health. I stopped laughing when I discovered that the person who wrote the series was the Prime Minister's nephew. It was probably all based on fact.

Just as we battle with our everyday relationships, so it is in political circles. The most important bond, if you are top dog, is the relationship that you have with yourself. There is no-one who is more important and there is no issue that is more significant than your re-election. Sure, there will be natural disasters, health epidemics and economic catastrophes and they will seem important at the time but having a firm hand on the wheel is an assurance of stability. I did mention the word destabilization earlier and this can wobble the wheels a tad.

Intervention can be quite destructive when it comes from within and this can often occur through a clash of dominant personalities. Usually, the winner is the most politically savvy.

My father, who was involved in local politics, used to tell me many hilarious stories about the continual conflict between one of the councilors and the Lord Mayor. The former lived in a new estate and had built a beautiful, state-of-the-art residence. It was the last home on a new road and because of his influence, a street that would obtain a priority paving contract. Unfortunately, public works was the Mayor's portfolio and his nemesis returned from leave to discover that the bitumen stopped at the penultimate house. The councilor, who was in charge of sewerage collection, retaliated in a predictable way but because of the respect I have for my young readership, the details will remain confidential. Nevertheless, quite funny!

Although impressed by my father's commitment to public life, I never harbored any desire to follow suit. I was too young to appreciate the fact that many of these vocations were based on the possibility that commercial benefits might accrue from elective power. Today, things have changed little and politics is a hotbed of back scratching and productive posturing. As we move higher into a more sophisticated arm of government, acolytes and lobbyists appear from nowhere to flog their influence and availability.

My dear departed dad was courted by the infamous John Wren and asked to join his political machine. Was this overture orchestrated because of his impressive record or because he was Irish? The boys from the bogs were a potent political force both in Australia and America and Wren was an artist in this early form of lobbying. He was a confidante of government ministers and the clergy and the fact that he ran an illegal betting establishment was of little consequence.

In the early part of last century, Catholics and Masons in Australia were to become dominant in a power struggle but both were easily outstripped by a much larger base of public opinion: Collingwood supporters.

If there is anything that makes a legislator mildly human, it is the fact that he or she supports the same football team as you and your family. Of course, this is beyond comprehension but so is reality television and haggis. People in parliament only embrace these kinds of ideals because they want to ingratiate themselves with you. You often hear the terminology *political football*, which usually relates to unresolved issues that are at odds with somebody or other. They bear no relation to a ball game and this remains so, even if someone takes up one of these issues and runs with it.

Voluminous literary accounts of this particular time in our history attest to the fact that Wren was closely aligned with this particular football club and the Irish population in general. In fact, one of my Irish relatives was the parish priest of Collingwood during this era and I still have Wren's condolence telegram, received after his death. I wonder if I should blame one of them for my unfortunate gambling habits.

You may think that I am drawing a long bow by bundling up all these old stories with a view to denigrating those who are committed to promoting our interests in a higher place. All right. I admit it. I would like to put a rocket up their ass and really send them to a higher place. For some reason, I have this affinity with situations that would look good on television.

Politicians like television, especially if they are on it. My message to you is: if someone asks you to vote for them, make sure that you thoroughly explore their credentials. Voters in America had the opportunity to put Dan Quayle or Sarah Palin within a heartbeat of the Presidency. If you are an Australian liberal, you have God on your side. The shadow cabinet boasts an Abbott and two Bishops.

IS THAT YOUR COUNTRY CALLING

I am not an authority on U.S. politics but I do live in a white house so that gives me some credibility. Of course, I am a realist and acknowledge the fact that the tenants of 1600 Pennsylvania Avenue are probably not that interested in getting together and comparing notes. A shame, really! I am sure that this power couple would be impressed by the humility of my lodgings and be amazed at the similarity to their own. You can almost land the Channel 9 helicopter on my front lawn.

I have always had a strange fascination with America's first family, irrespective of their political bent. The electoral process is pure theater and the preliminaries are totally absorbing. I find it rather amusing that so many people engage in such passionate rhetoric and in the end, many of them do not even vote. Where I live, voting is compulsory and we wouldn't have it any other way. In many third world countries, they not only insist that you lodge your preference but also help you make your mark. If you get it wrong, they may put you in a dungeon.

The democratic style is to have all these checks and balances: congressional approval, preferential voting, recounts etc. The ultimate fail-safe procedure is the election of a vice president — just in case the main guy doesn't make it through the night.

Did I say main guy? Tut tut. Where is my reasonable and impartial approach to gender equality? After all, the next American president will more than likely be a woman. I wonder if the current Secretary of State agrees. Mrs C is not quite there and may never be but there is evidence that a large part of the country thinks that it is time to bring a woman into the White House. This has been done before but I am sure that Hillary will insist on using the front door.

Bill could end up as the presidential handbag but I think that he can cope with that. More importantly, they will both be thinking *Dynasty.* Two Clintons would be no more than an empirical streak but you should never underestimate Chelsea. Once you get used to the West Wing, you never want to leave.

21

Hillary: The early years!

I don't mind a good dynasty and there has often been talk of a three-peat. Before things went pear-shaped, Florida's favorite son had serious presidential aspirations. Former Governor Jeb's financial qualifications didn't stack up and his brother's war on terror had put a huge dent in the economy. As one wag put it: *A third Bush in the White House wouldn't be much of a hedge against inflation.*

Reflecting on the Bush period, it is fair to say that Americans found it difficult to cope with two Georges and this is an indictment on everybody. In England, they are looking forward to George VII. Then again, nobody does nepotism better than a European monarch. Richard the Lionheart was followed by Richard III and this is where I think there could have been some common ground. Unfortunately, after Richard Nixon, nobody wanted to see another Dick unleashed in the Oval Office.

You can't talk American politics without a reference to the undisputed first family, the Kennedys. Why did so many of them aspire to the highest office in the land? Yes, they were pushed and prodded by their father but few would deny their leadership qualities. Sadly, only one of them made it to the top and not for long. Tragedy and natural attrition has seen family aspirations diminish and their time in the sun has gone. Nevertheless, these charismatic brothers had a real go at a dynasty. The Reagans had no chance. Ron Jr., was a ballet dancer and a confessed atheist.

People are not usually interested in my opinion but I like to give it. Right now, I am pretty hot for a female president in the land of the free. She would have to be an up-front kind of person: smart, charming, witty, and attractive. Someone like Dolly Parton! There is no point in electing Betty Beige and then spending heaps of taxpayer dollars to try and turn her into a colorful character. However, I am not locked into this way of thinking and there are other female role-models out there who would do just as well. I think that we would all be satisfied if the lady had all the virtues of somebody like Marge Simpson. She is not related to O.J. is she?

Vote for me.

Or somebody like me! I once had a friend who stood for public office. He was a bit of a greenie and his platform promises revolved around environmental concerns and animal welfare. He was devastated when the poll results came in. I felt obliged to feel sorry for the poor guy. Perhaps they could have included another box on the voting slip for creature comments? I'm sure that his dog and cat would have voted for him. That's what it is like when you are outside looking in. Even if you get in, you can't do much. You have no access, no influence and probably no idea. You may as well promise them the world and hope for the best.

Sometimes, I am so disillusioned by the whole political merry-go-round that I vote for someone who represents the lunatic fringe. I fondly remember a character in Britain called Screaming Lord Sutch, who campaigned in over forty elections. Sutch was a loony musician whose biggest claim to fame was his award for *Worst Album of All Time* in 1998. He was also a manic depressive and the great irony is that one of his successful opponents managed to obtain an increased budget for mental health. The screaming Lord may well have been the first patient in the new wing of the asylum.

In the country where I was raised, we adhere to the Westminster system of government. There is a sovereign who holds theoretical power over all but not much real clout. I hate that. It was a bit confusing in the old days because a sovereign was also a unit of currency. Awkwardness may also occur when the female ruler comes face to face with a queen of the male variety. The English language is so frustrating.

Right now, in an entirely different system, the American president is probably addressing the congress in an effort to have one of his nominated office bearers confirmed. On the face of it, he is probably a down-home kind of fellow but they still want to know what's gone down with this dude: everything since his fourth birthday. They will probably discover that he has seventy-five outstanding traffic violations, has welched on a financial pledge to the Boy Scouts and has had relations in a toilet with somebody who wasn't a relation. The guy is a shoe-in.

In less developed countries, due process is a little different and democracy is nothing more than an idle dream. If they have chopped off your arm or leg for some indiscretion, you may regret missing that goal in the World Cup. That guy in the toilet would be in real trouble, especially as the appeal system usually follows the execution of the punishment.

Leaders who live in this world have many names, from brutal dictator to despot and the number one man always carries a big stick when seen in public. Anthropologists remain impressed that tyrants have been able to slow the population explosion of their countries without resorting to birth control. It is actually called Death Control but you needn't worry unless you harbor opinions that differ from the boss.

In the introduction to this article, I chose to highlight an unsuccessful political power play by one of my friends. He was no despot and neither did he wish to be Prime Minister or President. This was local politics where you can be a complete bonehead and still get elected. Those of us who are cruel beyond comprehension never let him forget the fact that he was defeated in the first ballot.

If you are the lucky one that gets elected, you can almost feel those mayoral robes around your shoulders. This is a position that rotates every few years and gives you time to acquaint yourself with the burning issues that are important to your friends and neighbors. You will become an expert on urban renewal, kindergartens, waste disposal and everything to do with the Gay Pride march. If you are involved in awarding lucrative council contracts, it may be necessary to open a bank account in the Caribbean, just in case you want to holiday there or take advantage of one of those sister city junkets.

In recent years, my two closest boroughs have both been decimated by scandal and corruption and one involved the appointment of a white witch as a consultant. I think that everything would have been alright if she was black.

Now, I'm not the type of person to poke fun at our cherished institutions but there are others who are. One of the local columnists always refers to the municipality's monument to madness as the Clown Hall so you would have to think that this must be a fun place to work. Nevertheless, you can only stay in local government for so long. I suspect that our most recent Lord Mayor tired of wiping the rotten eggs off her doors and windows.

If you do mange to befuddle the voters and get elected, you may have to curb some of your less desirable habits. I can remember a local member who was let down by his own member. He was photographed entering the notorious *Pleasure and Pain Palace*, which was highly embarrassing. He maintained that he mistook the entrance for the grocer shop next door but this didn't help much. After investigation, the police discovered that this innocuous deli was the largest heroin outlet in the country. Eventually, the boys in blue solicited a confession from Madam Lash that the member had a loyalty card and many Frequent Crier Points.

Dare to dream.

Succession is a funny thing. Just because you are number two in the chain of command doesn't mean that number one is a comrade; even if he was best man at your wedding. The Ides of March comes around every year.

You may wonder why I highlight that infamous date in history when the previously noble Brutus plunged his dagger into Caesar's heart. Or was it his back? To be quite frank, that afternoon of the long knives was not a high point in the annals of the Senate. Why couldn't they have just given him a dressing-down over a nice salad lunch?

Just as the rule of law always invokes precedent, history is a memorial to things that have gone before and there have been a lot of nasty number twos' around. Once the leader hears public affirmation of support from his deputy, he knows that he is in trouble and his fears are probably well grounded. Ostensibly, if you've got the armed forces on your side, you've got the power. However, the generals can be fickle at the best of times and this is probably the worst of times. When your life partner decides to leave town without telling you, there is change in the air — especially if your joint account in that tax-free haven has also been plundered. It is hard to know what to do next. When the Chief Whip (Africa) asks for a meeting in his office, your whole life passes before your eyes. His office is in the basement for good reason. It is soundproof.

Ambition is such an unfortunate passion. You spend nine tenths of your life dreaming, scheming and manipulating yourself into a position of power. Along the way, you have destroyed your enemies, gutted your friends and irrevocably damaged most of your relationships. When you die, they will probably make a movie about your life. Posthumously, you will learn that John Malkovich has the leading role. What kind of tribute is that?

I could go on but I think that you get my drift. You can get yourself to the top of the tree but the buck stops there. The road to perdition is paved with deceit, disloyalty and degradation and once you reach the pinnacle of your power, there is only one way to go. Down, baby!

If you are presently recognized as a premium person with prospects, I hope my comments aren't off-putting in any way. The secret is to be bold and bolshie. Give no favors. Take no prisoners. At the end of the day, would I vote for you? Absolutely!

-3-

ENTERTAINMENT

On Broadway

The art of entertainment

Old Man River

I'm a bit of song and dance man, not that I sing and dance, myself. My generation prefers to shy away from the kind of displays that are currently presented on television talent quests. We tend to shrivel into a cocoon of complacency that can only be unraveled by a good revival.

Many of my entertainment pieces involve nostalgia and I feel that this is good practice for a time when I will have nothing but my memories.

I fear that this time is coming more quickly than anticipated as I seem to spend a lot of time in a comatose state. Nevertheless, I have retrieved any worthwhile material from my reveries and included them in my dispatches. I have saved my nightmares for another occasion.

ON BROADWAY

I love musicals. There, I've said it. Admittedly, my taste is a bit dated and I do insist that the score reverberate with harmony and the lyrics are clever and witty. That is why I just love *Guys and Dolls*. This durable masterpiece of sentimental schmaltz was based on the writings of Damon Runyon, another given in my literary hall of fame. The religious overtones of the production also take me back to fond memories of a former girl-friend, a devout foot soldier of the Salvation Army. She could beat that big drum better than the Energizer rabbit.

The good thing about musicals is that they endure long after you have left the theater. You'll sing through your supper, rip off a soliloquy in the shower and croon contentedly during coitus. The trouble is that you just can't get those damn tunes out of your brain. Did I mention that there was something wrong with my brain? I just can't seem to partition all my input into the right compartment. This makes me a very imaginative sleeper which can be a little awkward when I doze-off on the train.

Welcome to my dream. I had left Broadway and the after-party behind and yours truly was now rattling along on the subway, bound for a feather bed of exquisite comfort. The stray copy of the International Herald Tribune had been abandoned by a departed commuter. For those of you who are not familiar with this particular broadsheet, it provides a potted version of events on the world stage.

Being a shallow kind of person, I opened up on the sport page, looked for the comics and finally settled on the latest tittle-tattle from the movie world. I vaguely remember taking in details of Frank Sinatra's latest film project and an almighty row that he was having with his new wife, Mia Farrow, concerning her career choices. He wanted her for his new crime movie and she was itching for *Rosemary's Baby*. As my eyelids slowly dipped into listless inactivity, I managed one last glimpse as the underground darkness flashed by. My concentration was not required. The train just hurtled into the night.

Tony Rome was a world weary cop who had been on the 'Frisco beat long enough to be unfazed by anything. Nevertheless, he was surprised to get a semi-anonymous tip from a loud broad called Adelaide. She had credible information that there was going to be an evening of illegal gambling in a Broadway sewer. Even three thousand miles away, our boy knew that the game was usually held at the back of the police station. He was intrigued.

Rome was attached to the same precinct that employed Dirty Harry and although their budget was continually under pressure with vehicle replacements, mortuary over-runs and third party liability claims, the Captain had sprung for a return trip to the Big Apple. Contrary to television perceptions, inter-office jealousies rarely interfere with legitimate law enforcement and so it was that the combined forces of New York and San Francisco descended on the sewer in question and arrested one Nathan Detroit.

He was arraigned the next morning in District Court and charged with loitering with intent, promoting a crap game and singing off-key. His mouthpiece managed to produce twenty-seven character witnesses from the local chapter of the Salvation Army. Unfortunately, they all had records and none of them were in the music business. These guys and dolls weren't contrite sinners but fair weather friends and Nathan was in trouble — in more ways than one!

After a courtship lasting fourteen years and many tears, he had finally committed to Adelaide and weddings bells were imminent. Benny Southstreet was providing the getaway vehicle and Minnesota Fats was lending them his house and pool for the honeymoon. There was just one problem—the court appearance. Obviously, Judge Della Ware was a romantic or just didn't want to rock the boat. She let Detroit off with a good behavior bond. Approached by a court reporter, Tony Rome was brutally Frank and told the scribe to rack off.

Shake, rattle and roll! This was the subway as I knew it. There was never enough time for a kip. The slamming of the train brakes brought me back to reality and then I was catapulted into the arms of a shocked spinster who was sitting in the opposite seat. She blushed, smoothed out her skirt and promptly departed at the next station. I returned to my newspaper, still open at the entertainment page.

Dawn French was doing stand-up at the Paris Hilton and Victoria De Los Angeles was booked for the Opera House. As I was destined to become a great fan of *The Sopranos*, I made a mental note to try and get some tickets. My Spanish friend Andrés Segovia had always claimed that he could pull a few strings if ever I wanted concert seats.

I have always enjoyed music and remember with great affection, Dinah Washington and Alison Durban, who may not have come from South Africa and Florida's favorite son, Tony Orlando. The English had David Essex and Julie London but as Australians, we have nothing to fear from this type of rivalry and can be justifiably proud of our home grown talent. Alice Springs is more than holding her own in the competitive world of adult entertainment.

They say Joe Montana was the greatest quarterback ever. Those folks who lived around the Yellowstone River would never argue with that one. John Denver put it on the line for Colorado and in Sri Lanka, Colombo is renowned as the greatest detective of all time. What can you say about someone who gives up their own name in order to promote their home town or country? No wonder Cuba Gooding Jr., smokes big cigars and anyone with half a voice in Indonesia calls himself Frank Sumatra. So, how petty was John Wayne? He changed his name just because he was christened Marion.

Hello! What have we here? The Tribune has a gossip column. Not before time. I don't know about you but when I read reports about famous people and the shenanigans that they get up to, it really gets my heart racing. I know that they breathe the same air as we do and they put their pants on the same way but we really do need to know when and where they take their pants off. There was no better reporter of this genre than Louella Parsons. She had a nose for a good story but had serious competition from her rival, the habitual Hedda Hopper. When Hedda smelt the scent of scandal, nothing could stop her. Of course, neither of these ladies worked for The Tribune so the content was rather mundane.

I read that some Hollywood big wheels turned out for a knees-up with the Teamsters Union and the photo-op said it all. There was Van Johnson, Glenn Ford, William Holden and Chevy Chase, all smiling for the camera with the redoubtable Jimmy Hoffa. He would never smile again. A few days later he disappeared permanently.

The big news was that Ginger Rogers had dumped Fred Astaire and was now linked to one of the Spice Girls. This was denied by her agent but all the same, it was hard to keep up with all the bed-hopping of the rich and famous. Jack Lemmon was a billboard icon but he was upstaged by a bit player from Orange County, who won the heart of the latest hot tomato, Virginia Mayo. Fair suck of the sav; these people must do all their romancing in the supermarket.

By the time that the silver bullet finally arrived at my stop, I had overdosed on gossip and thankfully, that was the end of The Tribune. A cool wind arrived with the opening of the doors and the perceptive periodical was strewn all around the carriage in disarray. The docile dog that entered with the blind man had gone crazy and further contributed to the carnage. He must have been hungry for news. The doors closed, the train departed and I sauntered off down the platform whistling one of those great tunes from *Guys and Dolls*. I just couldn't get it out of my mind.

THE ART OF ENTERTAINMENT

The other day, in my local shopping precinct, I discovered that our classic bluestone thunderbox had been replaced with a talking toilet. A toilet with technology! When you first arrive, a welcoming voice tries to put you at ease with a risqué joke but it soon turns nasty. In a booming voice that can only be described as confrontational, you are instructed to do your business efficiently, flush quickly and not be wasteful at the wash basin. I thought that the soap dispenser was particularly bossy but if you didn't do what it said, they wouldn't let you out. You can't argue with these people and I felt totally stupid that I even tried. After all, it was just a recording. Eventually, the dead bolts were released and I staggered out into the fresh air but not before I did a double take. I recognized that voice.

Only a few nights earlier, I had been dragged, kicking and screaming, to a local production of Shakespeare and guess who was performing the dagger speech from Macbeth? I do have a good ear and I am pretty sure that the Nazi storm-trooper from the can and the Shakespearian thespian were one and the same.

As my escort was related to one of the witches in the play, I used all my renowned guile and tact to submit an enquiry. *Tell me, all knowing one. The overbearing lead actor from that tragic performance, the other night; does he do toilet humor on the side?* Surprisingly, I didn't get the two minute stare, which usually allows her time to formulate a suitable sarcastic response. Evidently, the person in question does moonlight as a voice-over man and the rest of the cast had already *taken the mickey*. There were similar toilets all over town.

For love or money!

Here's something. It turns out that acting professionals perform theater for love and anything else for money. This includes being a sperm donor or the inside man in a Huckleberry Hound costume. Both of these pursuits can be done anonymously. More common is the use of their dulcet tones to promote and endorse. However, there is still a degree of hierarchal pretentiousness involved and you don't expect the big guy to be working the basement. A few years ago, I was lucky enough to attend the Academy Awards in Los Angeles. When I returned to my hotel, I discovered that the winner of the best actor statuette was also Elliott the Elevator.

I have been involved in some of these types of productions and I have to say that both Romeo and Juliet are happy to take the money but not always appreciative of the simplicity of the task. They may have a point. Elevators are pretty boring. You are either going up or down and the journey can sometimes be a drag. Why not use gifted people to entertain the passengers? Perhaps *Richard III*, something from *Ocean's Eleven* and *Executive Suite* for the top floors?

The key to all this is that you probably need to be a baritone. Stern, authoritarian voices are always in great demand and are often used by utility companies in marshalling wayward commuters and destabilizing rebellion. *Stand behind the line. The next tram is not taking passengers. The 5.45pm train has been cancelled.* If are you a serious actor with great expectations, you should never accept a role as a fluffy animal. Mickey Mouse, Donald Duck and Bugs Bunny had longevity but their alter egos were buried in obscurity. Did you ever see Mel Blanc doing Hamlet?

It's a different story, if you have already achieved fame. A starring role in Shrek or a guest spot with the Simpsons is not too bad for the CV. If you've got a good voice, you don't need a good body. That's why they invented radio. Those soothing tones and modulated moans of licentious Lucy, from the late night show, will only continue to excite you if you remain ignorant of the fact that she is many pounds overweight, height deficient and has more chins than the Hong Kong telephone directory.

As technology takes hold and Hollywood merges with the corporate world, those inert household appliances that we take for granted are taking on a whole new life and personality. For a number of years, I have been talking to flowers and plants and other indolent members of my household. Now, the machines are talking back to me. My DVD player says hello and goodbye and my printer won't shut up. Specific kitchen appliances are in my face with a cacophony of sounds that always seem vaguely familiar. I suspect that my toaster is related to a small robot in Star Wars but I don't know on which side. I could go on forever about this but I can hear the kettle whistling. I wonder if Agatha Christie's estate has considered taking legal action against Russell Hobbs. It sounds very similar to the Orient Express to me.

The action attractions!

I am one of those people who are not blessed with natural talent. I would love to be able to whizz through a Chopin concerto or an aria from *Il Travatore* but as both would require immense dedication and patience, I defer to practicality; preferring instant gratification from low brow amusement options. However, I do owe my friend's friend an apology for snoring through their version of *Macbeth*. I don't know what came over me.

You could never snore through a Hitchcock film. I can remember the first one that I ever saw: *Strangers on a Train*. You may recall the finger-biting finale, where the action revolved around an out of control, manic merry-go-round. When the suspect made a lunge for one of the galloping horses, Sgt Plod grabbed his standard issue side-arm and fired at him, impervious to the collateral damage that might occur. I might add that the suspect had not been charged and was subsequently exonerated. Fortunately, he missed the kiddies on the ride but mortally wounded the elderly operator who fell onto the controls, thus sending the rotary conveyance into accelerated spin mode.

You just don't see that kind of stuff in the theater. Somebody should tell someone that you don't need a twenty minute speech before you pull the trigger. Just do it. Cut to the chase and hope that the hero or heroine will prevail, as they usually do. I think that most people applaud the victory of good over evil and if it can be done without brutality and violent behavior, all the better. Sam Spade never needed to resort to violence and Philip Marlowe didn't like to carry a gun because it crumpled his suit. James Bond didn't worry about any of that. He used to swim in his tuxedo but it always looked great by the time he got to the casino.

Bond worked for the Secret Service. He could kill anyone he wanted and usually did. Is this too much for a pacifist like you? I mentioned to a friend that I thought Tarantino was too gruesome so he said "See Saw." I thought that it would be a young person's film. I was right. They loved it. I went straight to the pub and got legless.

Perhaps I am being a bit too critical. After all, those cowboys used to blast everyone in sight and there was never any environmental or ethnic sensitivity, either. If there were Indians in the movie, they were there for the shooting. I really loved those grand old steam trains that used to service the Old West, especially that one with that huge frontal trellis. It was the Atchison, Topeka or the Santa Fe; or was it the Chattanooga Choo Choo? And how good were the passengers? With their trusty Winchesters, they could hit a rampant Apache, whilst traveling at speed.

Recently, I was drawn back to this era, when, in my local video shop, I happened upon a sublime double cassette. It offering thirteen episodes of *The Black Widow*: a tense, electrifying serial of the time. In those days, movies were awe-inspiring. Adults enjoyed a double feature and on Saturday afternoon, the kids devoured two cartoons, a serial and a western, starring one of Hollywood's great cowboys, of which there were many. Although the sets were a little fragile, the script terrible and the acting woeful, these deficiencies were overlooked because there was more action per minute than anyone could ever hope for. The heroes were adventurers and the crooks were nastiness personified.

The Black Widow made Lucrezia Borgia look like the fairy on the Christmas tree and there was none of that mushy romantic trash. The finale to every episode offered a calamity guarantee, which would bring the punters back next week. To this day, I don't know how Rex Wonderful was able to cut poor Mabel free from the train tracks in time. I wasn't around for *Dr Fu Manchu* or the *Perils of Pauline* but my parents were and they also swooned and salivated over those stars that came out of the studio system in Hollywood — Barrymore, Flynn, Bette Davis and even Ronald Reagan. Reagan was so popular, they made him President. I know that when I was a lad, I couldn't imagine anyone making a better president than Hopalong Cassidy. I still think it was a shame that he was passed over.

Botanical!

I have already mentioned my unfulfilled desire to make my mark at La Scala or Covent Garden, although it doesn't necessarily have to be *Il Travatore*. I think that I would have liked to do justice to *O Sole Mio* and make the late Luciano Pavarotti extremely jealous. I would do it without the handkerchief. Of course, some of you will be a little incredulous. It does seem a quantum leap from the Warner Bros back-lot to one of opera's hallowed halls of history.

The other day, I found a tenor in the park. He was mid-way between the azaleas and the roses and was propagating snatches of Bizet, Puccini and Donizetti. They were only snatches because this was some sort of voice exercise or else he was an eccentric, craving attention. It's probably a bit disconcerting, having only deciduous plants for an audience but he relished their attention and I'm sure they thought he was bloomin' marvelous. I certainly did and as I slowly munched on my bacon and baloney sandwich, my mind went back to that notorious advertising campaign that had set back the opera community about thirty years.

In those days, I was a supremely confident kind of guy. If you asked me, I reckon I would have backed myself to sail a sieve to Sweden. Otherwise, I would have never taken on such a challenging task. My client came to me with a brief to take opera to the masses. Part of his strategic planning was to market the whole damn thing in English. Now, I remember when the Catholic Church first went linguistic. The top brass changed the mass from Latin to English and there was uproar. They eventually smoothed the waters but taking the Italian out of opera is something else, again. What's linguini, if it's not spaghetti?

Nevertheless, I reached into my bag of tricks and came up with what he wanted. Unfortunately, Joe Green's *The Woman who Strayed* didn't have the same ring to it as Giuseppe Verdi's *La Traviata* and so the production went belly up. I also think that some people confused Joe Green with Moe Green, who was the gangster that was shot in the eye in *The Godfather*. I can't remember who my godfather was but my old man, the tax accountant, always used to say: "It is time to render to Caesar the things that are Caesar's." It was never time to take opera away from those who cherish it most, be they Romans, Milanese, Calabrians or Sicilians.

What about the artists, themselves? They were all larger than life. Luciano is no longer with us but they used to say he was eating too much *Rigoletto*. Not so. Big is beautiful and the airlines loved him. He always had to buy two seats. The competition is pretty serious south of the border and José and Placido are pretty happy guys but being number one is all important in a business where ego is everything. It is the same with the ladies. Wasn't it one of those early impresarios who decreed that the Prima Donna should be forever etched into operatic tradition as the best of the best? If she happened to be a little tempestuous, troublesome, vain, tardy, aggressive and slightly intoxicated, well, that was just icing on the cake. The names just roll off your tongue: Maria Callas, Sutherland, Tebaldi, Albanese and the first international African-American PD, Leontyne Price. The price must have been right the night she a received a forty-two minute ovation at the Met.

The last word on opera is always about first nights. It is essential for anyone with any kind of social standing in the community to be there. Wives will tuck their husbands into penguin suits with the promise that they can have a nap sometime during the second act. Celebrated composers like Puccini were awake to this kind of thing and produced arias like *None Shall Sleep*. If you've ever heard *Nessun Dorma*, you'll know that nighty night is not an option.

OLD MAN RIVER

I have a friend who thinks that he is black. Nobody else sees it that way; possibly because of his ginger hair, freckles and ruddy complexion. My buddy has previously received page space in this epic epistle: the one we call The Smarmy Red Ferret. I suppose if you don't put too fine a line on it, the battling baritone could be classified as an entertainer because every Saturday night he used to be found, front and centre, at one social function or another. *Tote dat barge. Lift dat bale. Git a little drunk and you land in jail.*

That old man river rolled around our town for about ten years and the suburban soloist never tired of tickling the tonsils just one more time. If asked, he would follow up with his rendition of *Danny Boy.* He was rarely asked and it was up to me, the stooge, to drum up support. I would enthusiastically call for an encore, at which time stooge number two would chime in with: *No, No! Let the same bloke sing again.*

It is strange how the lyrics of songs will wash over you and you rarely give them a second thought. When *Show Boat* first opened on Broadway under the guiding hand of the conspicuous Florenz Ziegfeld, there was great consternation and public outcry over racial sensitivities, especially concerning the show stopper *Ol' Man River.* It would be no different today and I can see howls of protest coming from so many minority interests. The senior citizens would object to the ageing connotations in the title and the feminist lobby would be equally outraged. *If this wasn't a female river, why did they call it the Mississippi?* Of course, the Longshoreman's Union wouldn't be far behind. What is minimum wage for barge toting, these days?

At the revival in our city, the singing stevedore was always working overtime. The production was running six nights a week plus a matinee on Wednesday and Saturday. The young and beautiful Magnolia puckered up to the debonair Gaylord Ravenal in over three hundred and seven consecutive performances. Off-stage, the chemistry was less than chummy. The leading man's advances were rejected because of the fact that he had a wife and four children. Men can be beasts, can't they? In retaliation for his rebuff, the river boat gambler made a point of consuming his pre-show dinner at *The Green Frog*, a French restaurant not far from the theater. He always ordered the dish with the most garlic in it.

Thespians always suffer for their art and Lily was a real trouper. You would expect it. She came from a showbiz family. Well, more or less! Her old man, who surely must have come from old Blarney, always maintained that he played the *Old Vic* back in the old country. When the scrap book was finally produced, it transpired that he played Victor Lazlo in a college production of Casablanca. Isn't it amazing how one's achievements are magnified as time goes by? When Lily auditioned for *Show Boat,* her scrap book was as devoid of achievement as that of her father but she lived for the theater and resided in a rental property not far from the theatrical district.

As the young lady really didn't have much money, you may wonder who was subsidizing the rental property. She had a mentor and it was this person who recommended her for the try-out. Since time immemorial, talented artists have been able to rely on their rich patrons. It gives you the opportunity to concentrate on your craft and be completely impervious to mortal considerations such as food, clothing or who is going to pick up your tab at the local pub. Lily's benefactor was an elderly supporter of the arts who had no children of his own and had too much money to give away. He set her up and under his patronage she performed and prospered. There would be few who were not captivated by her infectious personality and angelic singing voice. I have to admit that I was completely smitten myself when I first met her at the audition. Now, I know what you are thinking. How did I get in? Wasn't there anyone on the door?

In point of fact, I was there on behalf of The Ferret. There are few radical thinkers in this business and I always like to push the envelope, where possible. Let's dump the black guy and replace him with a red-head. In that way, I reckoned that we could appeal to the Irish locals and overcome all those racial issues. Let's face it. We have got ourselves into a big hole with all this political correctness rubbish. I even suggested that we write a Mississippi version of Danny Boy. The Ferret was keen but nobody else.

On reflection, controversial issues have never really bothered me and I doubt that I would have bought into the hullabaloo in 1927. No, I wasn't around to see Paul Robeson showcase his talent but I have enjoyed the *Cotton Blossom's* journey of delight on a number of occasions. This musical remains one of my all-time favorite shows. Perhaps it is not so co-incidental that the original book was penned by one of my favorite authors: Edna Ferber. The lady was the real trail-blazer of her time and specialized in historical epics relating to territorial awakenings such as the opening up of Oklahoma, Texas and Alaska. She was a Pulitzer Prize winner and received this accolade even before she produced the likes of Cimarron, Giant and the Ice Palace.

I don't have a lot of contacts in the publishing world. I wonder if it was something I said. My friends in show business are legion. We often catch up for a coffee and a natter — usually after their fortnightly visit to the dole office.

Unfortunately, some of my contemporaries are a little picky and have even been critical of some aspects of this Jerome Kern production. For instance: *How do you tap-dance on a boat?* This came from an idiot who couldn't tap-dance on land. There was also some argument concerning the derivation of the child's name, Kim. It is supposedly a modern christening but in point of fact, Rudyard Kipling's hero of the same name first appeared in 1901. The storyline of *Showboat* specifies that the tyke was born at the exact moment that the vessel bridged the watery junction of Kentucky, Illinois and Missouri. Only a writer with real imagination could come up with crap like that.

–4–

SPORT

Jiminy Cricket

What is there to like about football

Horse Tales

Australians don't like sport. We love it. If you are not so inclined, there is probably a fast-forward button somewhere.

This compendium of essential information will be heading stateside and I thought that I might attempt to help our American friends broaden their horizons. Cricket is a challenge for the uninitiated and it will be difficult to explain. However, football is ever-present in most societies and horse racing is the Sport of Kings. I won't hear a word said against it.

As a long-standing owner of thoroughbreds, my colors are always running. If you are reading this potboiler in Kentucky or Newmarket, you may feel a sense of compatibility. The rest of you will be smug in the realization that you are richer than we are.

JIMINY CRICKET

I have a friend from Boston who is an absolute sports freak. He is a bit of a clever clogs and can tell you Babe Ruth's batting average, John McEnroe's favorite swear word and the underwear size of the Patriot's Tight End. Now, I have to admit that I don't know what a Tight End is and this delights him considerably. Conversely, I also like to confuse the cocky son of a bitch and last Christmas I gave him a CD of famous cricket songs.

If you ever want to see an American take a backward step, bring up the subject of cricket. This is a game that they don't understand and are gobsmacked when you tell them that the contest can last for five days without a result. Even in those glory years of bare knuckle boxing, a bout never lasted longer than two days.

Nevertheless, Barry from Boston is also a music lover and music is a medium of simple pleasure. You can sing along to a catchy tune without needing to understand its meaning so I think my CD will find some airplay. I love it. In fact, I am humming one of the songs right now. *Howzat! You messed about. I caught you out. Howzat!*

The riff kind of gnaws away at you and the lyrics are rather banal and repetitive but multi-dimensional in a clever kind of way. The double entendre that links infidelity and cricket was prophetic. I wouldn't be surprised if they released a golf CD, this year.

The title of the song "Howzat" is akin to what members of the union movement call an ambit claim. What it means is *Hey, Mr Referee! That deceptive curve ball, which I threw up into the wind, trapped him leg before wicket. Is he out?* If the umpire concurs, his finger will be raised to the heavens amidst great relief, disbelief, joy or consternation, depending on which team you represent. The fact that his digit is only forty five degrees away from being an obscene gesture will not be lost on those viewing the game for the first time.

My friend Barry also goes on and on about baseball and the World Series. The World Series! Give us a break. The sport is hardly played outside Uncle Sam's boundaries. The game that is truly international is cricket. In India it is a religion and everybody gets involved: Hindus, Christians, Muslims and Sikhs. One of their great spin bowlers is called "The Turbanator" aka Harbhajan Singh. Nine months after he spun Australia to a humiliating defeat, the Census Board of India reported the arrival of five million new babies called Harbhajan. Being true blue affable Aussies, we took the defeat philosophically and why not? We were Punjabbed in the park.

Of course, England is the home of cricket and they like to make a real day of it. There is lunch, tea and drinks, if it gets too hot (over twenty degrees centigrade). The supporters applaud when you are in and they applaud when you are out. It is all very civilized. That is until the Australian lads arrive on the scene: their arch enemy. In 1882 these two teams faced up to each other at The Oval in London and the unthinkable occurred. Australia won the match. At the conclusion of the game, they burned the bails and instigated this perennial rivalry known as "The Ashes." Those ashes remain in a small urn, the size of your finger and there is always a degree of hostility between the two nations when the fire dust is up for grabs. No quarter asked. None given. I would cite the American Civil War or the Coke/Pepsi conflict as a comparison. You know what I mean.

When I first heard Harry Belafonte sing the Jamaica Farewell, I wanted to go there — especially when I learned that they all loved cricket in the West Indies. Then along came Bob Marley, Reggae music and Usain Bolt. What a great place. You can sit down with a beer and watch the fastest man in the world or the slowest game on earth. This is what they call a Dreadlock Holiday and I reckon that even Boston people must have heard of that. The *10cc* version peaked at #44 on the Billboard Top 100.

Playing the game! Ask someone who knows.

Before you can even think about participation, you need to acquaint yourself with the correct terminologies and there is no finer reference than *The Wisden Book of Cricket* aka *The Bible*. You will discover that the basic edicts are simply enough. Face every day with a straight bat and avoid hookers. It's almost a directive for life, isn't it? They should have called it *The Wisdom of Cricket*. I do know that if you've got a short leg, you'll probably have a few slips — especially, if you get caught in a gully! You can score with a tickle behind leg but with no balls, you can't bowl a maiden over. Fairly straightforward, really.

Cricket enthusiasts are always deep thinkers and I cannot speak too highly of their desire, commitment and sense of fair play. They are also so meticulous. They can tell you who caught who on the second day of the first test at Trent Bridge in 1897. Don't even bother to ask why they would play a test match on a bridge. I'm from the colonies and we have been engaged in sporting combat with our masters for over a hundred years. It would be nice if the reward could be a swag of diamonds or something that is gold or silver but alas, you have already heard that the treasured prize is a small urn, full of ashes. This does becomes quite practical if the dressing room microwave goes down because sometimes there are a lot of ducks about.

If you fail to score you are deemed to have made a duck. Your team mates will probably think that you are just a silly goose. Evidently, the zero numeral that they include in the records for posterity resembles a duck's egg. I think that the birds should cry foul. If you have ever tried to pass a round egg, you would know that it is a painful experience.

It would be remiss of me if I failed to complete this totally absorbing commentary without reference to those who have played the game and covered themselves with glory. The honor board of past and present players is long but because of my renowned attention deficit problems, I can only remember Gillie, Lillee, Willy and Dilly. Mr Gilchrist was a wicked keeper and the others were just plain nasty in a bumper era for fast bowlers. Everybody remembers Warnie. He's the spin bowler with more front than a rabbit with a gold tooth. In his test debut against England, he produced what is commonly referred to as "the ball of the century."

Gatting was batting when Shane spun out of control. He flipped, dipped and doodled his way into the annals of sporting history. Such a nice guy. He even sent a sympathy text message to Mr Gatting at the *Asylum for the Bewildered* where he now resides with his memories. The blond bombshell has now retired but what a legacy he leaves behind. Three years ago, one of my best pals couldn't stand cricket. Now his two sons are called Shane 1 and Shane 11.

You're a Yankee Doodle Dandy.

Of course you are. Probably even born on the 4th of July. Did you know that the British were possibly playing cricket on your patch while you were loading your muskets at Valley Forge? Why on earth didn't you embrace the game in its infancy? Perhaps George Washington made a duck and stormed off in a huff. This entertaining pastime has been around for quite a while but few would know that the first ever international match was actually played in New York in 1844.

I have to be honest. I didn't know this, myself. I looked it up. In fact, I don't know much early American history, at all. Somebody told me that Peter Stuyvesant introduced cigarettes to America and he faced stubborn opposition from the Duke of Marlboro. Strangely, I have never been able to substantiate that information, which is probably down to sloppy work by the historians. This is where the cricket historians are way out in front. They have chronicled every single ball that has ever been bowled in the history of the game. They put these little dots down on paper as it happens. Well, actually, they put the dot down when nothing happens and that is most of the time. With such perfect records, you can look up the last over on such a day of such a test and say: *There you go. I've won my bet. He bowled a maiden over.*

Now, I know what you're thinking. He's bowled a maiden over. Call in the Hill St Blues and five years without parole. I can understand your anger because such creatures are hard to find but you are way off the mark. If you bowl six balls at your opponent and he doesn't score, that is classified as a maiden. It is derived from medieval Saxon times. If you couldn't score after six attempts at unlocking her chastity belt, the lass retained her maiden status. Makes sense to me.

The end game!

I could go on and try and explain the psychology of cricket but I am worried about your sanity. I have given you a lot to think about in one sitting and quite frankly, you may have jumped out the window fifteen minutes ago. I do hope that you live at street level. Certainly, cricket is not for everyone and it was never meant to be. The British Raj couldn't conceive that Elephant Boy would one day wield the willow spectacularly and those toffs at Eton and Cambridge were equally elitist. They nearly choked on their chowder when they heard that those convicts in Australia had taken up the game. Perhaps because we were convicts, we played the game with such conviction. It has taken us to the top of the tree and the contest enthuses young and old and everyone has an opinion. How democratic is that?

I didn't want to bring politics into this little chinwag but we all know that even our most un-athletic leaders will shamelessly rush to support our sporting heroes because of the game's international credibility and media attention. Such is the power of cricket. In truth, they are probably as confused as a frog in a sock. Even our troops embrace every opportunity to release their tension with a game of cricket. Yes, they carry their fragmentation hand-grenades, assault rifles and their service pistols but look closely — there's always a long handle Kookaburra sticking out of one of those backpacks. It can come in handy when your rifle jams and you are out of grenades.

WHAT IS THERE TO LIKE ABOUT FOOTBALL

I'm glad you asked. Football is one of the most popular recreations in the world and continually excites, irrespective of code or country of origin. It is a true gladiator sport that is played by both sexes and the professionals showcase their skills in an amphitheatre that is nothing less than a cauldron of mass hysteria. The screaming, vociferous fans direct their invective at all and sundry but particularly at those who are obliged to referee the contest. It is a brave person who thinks that they know more than a totally biased and uncompromising fanatic but umpires have little choice. They were never good enough to play the game themselves but they need a stress release, away from their daily routine as pedophiles and sheep-shaggers.

When my parents sent me to a boarding school run by religious zealots, I suppose that it was inevitable that I would be asked to renounce Satan at an early age. I was told that he could manifest himself as anyone he wanted but nobody mentioned that one of his incarnations was that of a football umpire. I learned that for myself.

It is difficult to understand why so many of us have such a competitive nature and the passion that is channeled into this particular recreational sport is right up there with your first Barbara Cartland novel. I would say that it almost defies analysis except that is what I am here for. There are four major football codes on this planet and I just know that you will be fascinated by my take on them all.

Soccer

The world game! The beautiful game! Call it what you will but it is certainly bigger than *Ben Hur*. I must admit that I am amazed that the wheels haven't fallen off. After all, it is a tad slow and overly theatrical. Yes, I'm talking about diving, falling, collapsing and any other self-propelled journey to the ground that seems to occur every five minutes. A little ankle tap and all of a sudden it's the Battle of Wounded Knee. Where do they recruit these agony aunts — NIDA? Certainly, some of them would not be out of place, clutching a small statuette on the stage of the Kodak Theater in Los Angeles.

As I write this penetrating dissertation of the round ball game, my country will be embarking on another tilt at their most elite competition. For the most part of every year, the World Cup is on everyone's lips and if this isn't a poisoned chalice, I don't know what is. I was quite bemused when our lads returned home from Germany to an assessment that the net result was good even though we didn't score many goals. I think I might pass that appraisal on to Price Waterhouse for their comment.

The fascinating thing about our interest in international spectator sport is that we will embrace it, even if it isn't exciting: the ninety minute soccer game with no score is a perfect example. I think they erred when they passed over Sam Goldwyn as the first FIFA President. I recall one of his most admirable quotes: *Let's start the movie with an earthquake and move up to a climax.*

If you are an aficionado of soccer, you may become a little prickly when you realize that I have chosen to highlight the negative elements of this sport, in contrast to the thrill-a-minute spectacle that enthralls so many people around the globe. I suppose that they must be doing something right. Why else would any one match demand nine hundred minutes of analysis for every ninety minutes of game time? So, why is the game so beautiful? I decided to ask around.

Prince Charles preferred Polo and so did Ralph Lauren. Billy Connolly and Elton John both said *"balls"* but the latter used to own a soccer club. So did Anthony La Paglia and he's a Hollywood man. Isn't that where David Beckham used to live? Didn't I tell you that there was a direct link between acting and soccer? This game is also an excuse to print money. Clubs like Manchester United and Real Madrid are seriously solid and Russian billionaires who are ruble rich all want to buy a football franchise.

They will discover that winning a premiership is not a walk in Gorky Park, no matter how cashed up they are. It will, however, give them the opportunity to get people on the playing field whose skills are sublime and would be wasted in another country, playing for another team. This brings me to the likes of George Best, Diego Maradona and Edmundo the animal. These superstars have all been a delight to watch and nothing has impressed me more than their innate skill in being able to always absorb the pressure, when in trouble. They were also pretty good on the football arena.

In Australia, we are playing the game in a completely different environment to that which existed some years ago. The ethnic cleansing is over. The fire-bombs have been extinguished and the stadiums re-built. The surging A-league is ready to showcase our talent to the world and traditional rivalries are being replaced by international ones. Nevertheless, it will take some years to sow the same seeds of contempt that you need to promote really healthy competition. What can I say? Have I missed something? They still kiss each other whenever they score a goal and I can't pronounce any of their names.

Rugby

The Brits call it rugger. Well, they would, wouldn't they? If we are talking Union, I can tell you that it is the game that is played in heaven. I can't tell you who came to this conclusion but it does reek of bullshit. Certainly, this would not refer to games that are played Down-Under.

Australia has had a glorious history in this particular sport, until recently. First of all, along came a clown called Jonny Wilkinson, who never missed. He was from over there and he stole the World Cup from us. Then there was this New Zealander called Dan Carter, who never missed and a South African, who never missed. Color me bitter, if you like but how much can a koala bear? My goodness! I hope that I am not confusing you. We are actually called the Wallabies.

Our cousins who play in the international League competition are called the Kangaroos and we have various other outback marsupials who have gladly given up their name in the pursuit of sporting immortality. Unfortunately, most of them are very timid animals and are often scared off when those horrible Kiwis do their Haka before every game. This can be quite intimidating and sometimes our own coach gets in on the act. How would you feel about getting a tongue lashing before and after the game?

The supporters are not so timid. They will not only target their own players with the finger but the umpire, the opposition team, their supporters, the constabulary, the fire brigade and any other emergency organization that has been called in to quell dissent and reduce tension. They are very colorful in the use of the vernacular and also dress appropriately. I love those long gold scarves that double as a neck tourniquet, should the noise from the opposing supporters need to be quelled.

The aforementioned cousins are in a league of their own and prefer to make their headlines on the front page. Their sexual proclivities have been well documented and this is regarded as hard news because it is something that we want to know. Nevertheless, this kind of publicity is disappointing because the players are role-models to thousands of youngsters, who will live in their image. There is a certain morality that goes with being a role-model. The important thing is that fans get an opportunity to bond with their heroes but this adulation should not be carried too far. If there are any young girls out there who don't know the difference between bonding and bondage, I urge them to defer on the side of caution.

These kinds of side-issues are diversionary and I really don't know why I brought them up. It all comes down to game day and then it's over. The blood pressure has been up and now it is down. Some of the protagonists have enhanced their CV and you and I are secure in the knowledge that we are better than they are. It gives you a warm glow, doesn't it?

Gridiron

American football can be quite exciting, especially during the Super Bowl, which is a television feast for the whole nation. At the end of the day there will be much celebration and gnashing of teeth, depending on which side of the result you are sitting on. However, sometimes winning can be disappointing. I just love those cute cheer leaders but how do you get to kiss them with those ridiculous helmets in place?

If you appreciate rugby, you can probably pick up this form of football pretty quickly because it is a derivation of the same game. Wide receivers and goal kickers share similar functions and responsibilities but Rugby League people don't like to talk about any similarities to the previously mentioned offensive position known as Tight End. One of their players was recently sent to the sin bin for applying an on-field suppository.

A number of Aussies have made a name for themselves as punters and excited the fans with their ability to kick long and true. Such skill is not to be under-rated but they don't cut it with the quarterback, when the MVP awards are dished out. The names just roll off your tongue: Tom Brady, Joe Montana, Dan Marino etc. These luminaries were as slippery as an eel in Vaseline and could deliver bullet passes with pinpoint accuracy. I once saw the Bronco boys take on Dallas and the Cowboys' quarterback was awesome. My date, Debbie, certainly thought so. She went off to get his autograph and I didn't see her until three days later. In those days, Denver's defense was known as the Orange Crush and not to be confused with The Juice, one O J Simpson.

Orenthal James Simpson is a special person to me and not because he was a fine Running Back for the Buffalo Bills, an implausible actor or a convincing advertising spokesman. We actually share a birthday. Isn't that great? I don't know where he is, these days but I do know that he will be kind, loving and not even passively aggressive. That's what we Cancer people are all about but don't take my word for it. You can read it in my horoscope.

AFL

The Australian Football League is not an international competition and I think that is a shame. Compare the Olympics, for instance. The flame is carried from one country to another and even the rivalry to host the occasion is intense. We like to play hard ball but never dirty pool. When our dazzling demigod from Dandenong dons his green and gold Speedos, he'll be diving for a medal, not a yellow card. That's the kind of athlete we breed in this wonderful country of ours. The ones we import are good, too and people don't care if we can't pronounce their name. We'll just call them Aussie Vladimir and dream of Olympic glory.

Many of these competitors are household names in their very own household but relatively unknown beyond Bondi Beach. AFL is all about the home-grown athlete, although we do tolerate the occasional Irish presence. After all, these lads are part of our heritage and can stand up to the rigors of the contest, which is not put on for the faint-hearted. It is played without padding or any other protective gear.

This game is so tough I know that some parents are nervous of the physical implications and try and steer their babies into less demanding pursuits of a non-violent nature. You may be down in a croquet or lawn bowls tournament but nobody puts the boot in — perhaps a quick rabbit chop when nobody is looking but hey, are we competitive or what?

I am not calling anyone a wimp but we are talking credibility here. The AFL had their Mr Football and the fearless Captain Blood. Mr Ping Pong doesn't have the same ring to it. Anyway, these assigned embellishments are probably past their use-by date. The Lithgow Flash was fine for its time but today it would get you three months in jail. It's funny about names, isn't it? I can remember when I was a small boy and tennis stars Hoad and Rosewall were taking all before them. I thought his name was Lew Toad and that he played for France. I don't know where I got that from.

We all have our favorite teams and shamefully the teams we love to hate. I suppose that you can't write an article about AFL football without reference to the much loved/despised Magpies — the Collingwood Football Club. They have represented the working man since before the turn of the century and since that time have been the richest and one of the most successful clubs. In recent years, they have been disappointing and this state of affairs brings great joy to supporters of all other competing clubs.

When the black and white army gets their momentum up, we are all prisoners of their emotional juggernaut. Only when the last vestige of hope and expectation is crushed from their excitable bodies can we let out the snigger that we have long harbored in our hearts and souls. Even if your own team doesn't make that one day in September, a Collingwood loss makes up for everything. That's the kind of folks we are.

I think it irks us that they have supporters stashed away all around the globe — from bushwhackers to brain surgeons. In England, the Colliwobbles are almost as famous as the Teletubbies. However, I take some satisfaction in the fact that America's best golfer actually supports Richmond. Go Tigers. On the other hand, Truman Capote was famous for his black and white balls and unless you were American royalty, you had Buckley's chance of getting an invite. And Truman was keen. When the boys were over there for an exhibition match, they had to lock the doors to keep him out of the dressing rooms.

HORSE TALES

I don't want to sound in any way chauvinistic but isn't it true that we males are great providers? Even though Paul McCartney is no longer speaking to his ex-wife, he has provided for her every need for the next four hundred years. If you own a racehorse you will understand the comparison. The cost of every last oat and vitamin supplement plus the fees for his conditioning regime are put on my tab with never-ending regularity. Is it not fair to assume that you might expect some kind of enthusiastic commitment in return?

The other day, I asked one of my racehorses whether he was happy in the service. He snorted. Now, this is not an unusual reaction from my equine friend because he tends to snort quite a bit. Unless one is well versed in horse talk, it can be difficult to assess whether this communication transmits dissatisfaction, contempt, tiredness or sexual frustration. It was rather frustrating for me because usually I wouldn't have had the nerve to even consider questioning his desire and loyalty and that is exactly what I was doing.

He used to be a great racehorse and often he would delight his owners by appearing first at the finish line. Admittedly, his manners weren't always the best and I do regret that he head-butted the course photographer. Fortunately, the syndicate avoided a legal suit because no one had a pictorial record of the incident.

I don't know exactly when things started to go wrong but right now I could beat him. His inferior performance is also impacting on my own confidence and I fear I am fast becoming a figure of ridicule at the track. Whenever I walk through the betting ring, grinning bookmakers roll out his starting price. This is a difficult time for owners: the downward spiral. We appreciate the early successes and don't begrudge him his therapeutic treatments, podiatry and general grooming indulgences. However, I think that he now needs psychiatric help.

Many of us have been on the couch and it is no longer the social stigma that it once was. That aside, practitioners of equine psychiatry face a monumental challenge because some horses just don't have competitive natures. I would hate to be advised of this as they are lining up for the start of the Oakleigh Plate. Recently, I discovered that our poorly performed mare was a lover rather than a runner. The object of her affection was the horny Shetland pony from the adjoining paddock. Max is a pretty belligerent kind of guy but he is kind of short in the leg department.

In the meantime, therapy is still on the agenda for the gelding and I have to look him in the eye and tell him that someone is going to mess with his mind. It may be that some horses are sick of being conned. After watching the dish-lickers at Dapto, they could well surmise that the hare that always wins is rather light-on in the meat department and not worth chasing. Where are the rewards? As the two legged infidels divvy up five million big ones for the Melbourne Cup, they get two carrots and a stomach drench.

A horse's tale is never completely told at the racetrack but most of us don't really care because that's all we are interested in. Those who still have their goolies will discover life as a stallion. Mares will enjoy motherhood in a quite pasture.

Most of my racehorses have been geldings, who never knew what they had until they didn't have them. I wonder if his snorting is a result of bitterness. For the sake of your sanity and the pockets of the other owners, it is sometimes wise to move on. This will mean that the straw palace will be given over to another hopeful and the devoted strapper will bid a tearful adieu to her faithful companion, who has nuzzled and nudged her playfully for these past few years. She will be able to renew acquaintances occasionally, as he struts gracefully through the Moomba Parade, as a police horse. I hope his arrest record is better than his track record, which was hand-timed in a four horse race at Tatura, sponsored by the local abattoir.

There are some owners who don't see the need to move beyond the boundaries of the betting ring and the grandstand, which is a shame. Being close to the horse flesh will give you the realization that this is not an investment that derives all its pleasure from financial gain: there are stable visits, social occasions and bragging rights around the water cooler. Your neddy becomes one of the family. For this reason, I should tell you that all horses in this country celebrate their birthday on the first day of August. They prefer presents that they can eat and this includes vegetable matter, non-combustible grass and large hats.

By the way, do you want to know how my heart-to-heart with the horse went? The snort was of little consequence. You have to look into their eyes. This is where I go for guidance and affirmation. If he looks the other way, the kiddies' school fees are safe for another term. If he happens to wink at you; well, that's another story.

The Name of the Game!

The thing with love, marriage, birth and all that stuff is that you get to choose the name of your own child. Racehorse owners don't always have it so good. They sweat blood to come up with something original and clever and rush to the Registrar's office to proudly submit their chosen moniker. The horse couldn't care less. Her soul-mate and constant companion, the strapper, has already provided her stable name and the owners had no say in the process.

Strappers are typically female and usually in their early twenties. Thus, the nag tag is likely to be a tribute to the lass's favorite rock star or a peculiarity relevant to the horse's demeanor or physical appearance. My horses have been named after television shockers such as Ozzy and Jerry Springer and carried embarrassing names like Beatrice, Jade, Lurch and Knackers. Don't get me wrong. The owners do what they can but some of their best intentions can go awry due to the long lead-in process. Confidence and optimism are very meritorious qualities but the rule of thumb is to never call your colt *Lightning Jack*. If the steed persists in leaving the barrier five lengths behind the other competitors, you will end up with egg on your face.

Nevertheless, names need to be memorable. Tallulah Bankhead was an accomplished actor who performed on both sides of the Atlantic to great acclaim. On the billboards, there would only be one name that anyone would remember. How much harder do you think those early days would have been if her title had been plain Mary Smith? In the same era, the prolific author Daphne Du Maurier, gave us *Rebecca* and *Jamaica Inn*. Such a splendiferous appellation. It just rolls off the tongue. Nevertheless, her good father, the inimitable Sir Gerald, will possibly persist in posterity longer than she. An enduring limerick forever links him to a girl called Gloria and the band at the Waldorf Astoria.

I don't want to harp on this name thing too much because it can cause bad blood in the stable. I know that one of my steeds had a less than complimentary soubriquet for me but in all fairness, I only called him *Glue or Glory* as a motivational incentive. He was a very slow animal.

Of course, this is me all over. If I could possibly predict my own contribution to posterity, I would imagine that I would be forever linked to impossible racehorses and my irrational efforts to improve them. When I finally depart this life, I will not be surprised if it is courtesy of a hoof to the heart. Already this year, my equine employees have broken two bones in my foot, tried to sit on me and defecated on my best Italian brogues. One of my young colts also managed to scuttle a promising romantic attachment.

It was her ladyship's first visit to the track and during lunch she kept insisting that I get her a tip, straight from the horse's mouth. Those who have ever been close to that particular orifice would realize that it is not a happy experience. In retrospect, I should have been the harbinger of halitosis but, inexplicably, I playfully pushed her towards the foul-smelling animal. Witnesses have since claimed that I was wearing the hint of a smirk on my face, which I vehemently deny.

What happened next was something that you wouldn't wish on your worst enemy. As she gasped for air, shock and awe took over. Her knees buckled and those finely manicured fingers released their grip on her recently purchased Christian Louboutin clutch bag (retail $945) which dropped into a recently deposited mound of horse poop. On her way down, my favorite three-year-old took a fancy to her colorful Peter Jago designed fascinator (friend's discount $410) and helped himself to an ample mouthful. Need I go on? She hasn't spoken to me since and I blame the horse.

God only knows my name has been mud with so many women but Christ Almighty, let he who is without sin cast the first stone. When Irishman Dermot Weld stopped winning those Melbourne Cups, St Patrick's celestial supervisor changed his name to Allah and jumped onto the Darley bandwagon. Is this regarded as plagiarism? I remember they claimed that Sir Francis Bacon wrote Shakespeare's plays. Certainly, Hamlet was a bit of a giveaway.

I expect that there will be no confusion as to who wrote the nonsense that you are now reading. At heaven's gate, I hope to wake up from that fatal hoof to the heart and be welcomed by all the big names in horse-racing literature, from Damon Runyon to Dick Francis. I only hope that I don't meet any horses in heaven that should be in hell.

The Sales!

I always go to the yearling sales. There is nothing like the smell of money in the morning. Unfortunately, it is diluted by other extraneous smells that always occur when there are a few hundred horses assembled in the same place. However, this is not a distraction for the enthusiasts who are in attendance to interact with all members of the racing fraternity. The place is infected with breeders, trainers, vets, prospective owners and the media. A great networking opportunity. The only participants who don't want to be there are the animals and I can understand that. Their best friend is about to sell them for thirty pieces of silver and to the highest bidder, no less. Should I mention that they are prodded and poked at all day? As for those inspection walks — what a bore!

The Sheiks will bring their shekels and Australia's richest men will try and outbid each other for a three-quarter brother to a half-sister of an unraced relation to Phar Lap. The price tag will probably exceed three million dollars and the successful bidder will not be the least bit perturbed when his pessimistic financial advisor tells him that Nellie Melba's brother couldn't sing. I think that this comparison is a bit flawed. In fact, I often tell people that Dannii Minogue can sing just as well as her sister Kylie.

The fact of the matter is that bloodline shopping is the only real alternative to buying on type. Needless to say, both are inconsequential when compared to luck. We hear countless rags to riches stories and sporting history is well served with literary and celluloid depictions of these great moments in time. We hear less about all those people who have gone from riches to rags. This situation, my friends, far exceeds any other. I am not saying that the gentleman who outlaid the three million dollars for the yearling is heading for a fall but it is a worry when his trainer nominates the said animal for a maiden at the local picnic meeting. This is not a good sign.

In the sales ring, the auctioneer's incantations promise a climatic conclusion to the frenzied bidding war. However, the most sobering appraisal can come from a most unlikely source. My friend's six year old son piped up: *Daddy, why couldn't he buy a dog, like everyone else?*

I suppose that I should tell you that they were both there as novice on-lookers. In my naivety, I thought that they would be good company and generously invited them along. It didn't take long for skepticism to set in. We were only half way through the morning session when I was nudged in the ribs. Geoffrey needed to tell me that the clock on the wall had just bid forty thousand dollars for a beautiful chestnut filly.

Clocks are an important part of a filly's life. If she impresses those with the stop watches, she will be a lady with definite prospects. Being two lengths clear at the clock-tower at Caulfield is admirable and eventually the maternal clock starts ticking. Then, the cycle starts all over again. Of course, that beautiful foal is not always going to fulfill expectations. You might see a rather dejected figure at the bar drinking a non-vintage wine that tastes like vinegar. The pride of his life has just been passed in for fifteen thousand dollars. The service fee was thirty thousand and the upkeep and presentation cost another ten grand. It was a painful experience. When they were unloading the wretched animal from the float, she indicated her distain for the process by biting him on the ear. Female intuition, I expect.

Sitting beside him at the bar, the previously mentioned buyer and three of his friends have just demolished four bottles of French champagne to celebrate the three million dollar purchase. The pain intensifies when one overhears his supermodel companion confirm that they have a definite booking for the honeymoon suite at the Casino. The ignominy of all this is that two years later, the expensive colt has just won his maiden at Donald (on protest) and the realization sets in that he did buy a dog, after all. Not that he saw the race — he ran out of gas two miles short of the town. Donald, where's your bowsers?

Meanwhile, the filly already has three Group races to her name. Unfortunately, two weeks before she wins the season's classic two-year-old event, the breeder sells the filly to a mobile phone salesman from Niddrie, who thinks it would be a hoot to be horsey. The champion sprinter is now conservatively valued at five million dollars and is afforded every luxury. She even has her own mobile phone.

Don't think for a minute that I don't have a lot of sympathy for the poor codger who has to gamble on a feeling and then wait at least twelve months before he knows whether he has a good one or not. Was it Dr Doolittle who could talk to the animals? What an advantage that would be and so simple. The Sheik of Dubai rocks up to the sales complex and divulges to the much heralded occupant of stall seventeen that he is ready to part with two million big ones as an incentive to transfer to his A team. Is there anything that he should know?

Well, Mohammed says the colt. *That X-ray didn't pick up on my peptic ulcer and I still have a nasty itch in my crotch. Otherwise, I'm good to go.* Too easy, of course. People in our industry are renowned for doing the hard yards and where would we be without disaster, drama, doubt and disappointment? I have had my fair share. Once I scratched my head during a lull in the bidding and ended up with a half-brother to Radish or was it Mr Ed?

Those of you who are television aficionados with long memories will recall Mr Ed, the talking horse. Ed didn't talk for everybody but when he did he was full of sarcasm and cynical rhetoric. Battle-scarred punters and exasperated trainers have long felt the need to converse with their favorite animals on a more intimate basis and this gift of speech may eventually be ours to give. We have already produced the bionic ear and artificial hip so the virtual voice box can't be far away. I know that there will be conservatives in our industry who will urge caution in this area and I can understand why. Do we really need another opinion?

Back at the yearling sales, the sun sets on another day of wheeling and dealing and the key players draw breath and reflect on the state of their fortune or misfortune. Fortunately, their bank manager is on speed dial and takes after-hours calls. Down in the barn, tears are flowing as the young strapper sees her charge whisked away to who knows where. The new owners are paid up and proud and optimistically looking forward to Flemington and Cup Week. Aren't we all?

The Punt!

If you are a passionate member of the thoroughbred racing community, you are acutely aware of the speculative nature of the industry. The social order can be maintained without resorting to gambling but I like to think that the potential rewards are diminished considerably if one chooses to go down that path.

Yes, I do have a flutter and I am a bad loser. Scattered around my office are any number of diminutive horses, representative of my most unfortunate memories. They are actually soft toys but I use them as voodoo dolls. Of course, I only insert small acupuncture spikes. Except for one horse. For him, I utilize my late aunt's knitting needles. Some people might wonder why the intrepid owner/punter continues to butter up after he has been continually let down. Obviously, they are not party to the complicated post race review that takes place between the jockey and connections. There is always an excuse.

A horse race is sometimes seen in a different light, by different people, in different places. From the grandstand, you may feel that your colt has performed badly but on returning to scale, the small person will explain to you in great detail why it should have won by seven lengths. The animal may also have a viewpoint but if he lets go with a definitive neigh, this is not to be interpreted as a contradiction to the hoop's analysis. If the noise comes from the other end of the beast, that is a different matter.

Every week-end, I go to the track and put my trust in the little people. It's probably my Irish background. In all probability, the rider was in a difficult position. Whether he was there due to a bad barrier, a slow start or a tactical maneuver is irrelevant. It means that one has to make executive decisions, so they usually bide their time and wait for a gap to appear. This is called riding for luck and as soon as this phrase is muttered in any context, a collective groan is heard from trainers, owners and punters alike. As often as not, the opening appears and then disappears as fast as free beer. With it goes next week's rent money and the prospect of avoiding another embarrassing confrontation with a brutal loan shark.

I must say that I have had a lot of bad luck with jockeys. You may remember, a few years back, the lad who transferred from one horse to another during a race. He felt that that the other horse had a better winning chance. As one who had financially supported the empty horse, I was quick to question his loyalty. Unfortunately, he didn't have time to discuss the matter as he had a newspaper column to write and thousands of punters were awaiting his considered opinion. I was left contemplating the fact that jockeys aren't allowed to tip. Hello Integrity Services. Is anyone home?

If you sell tips to a person of ill repute in a sleazy Sydney night club at midnight, you will probably be warned off for life. Melbourne also has its underbelly but there's not much happening down there. A number of colorful racing identities are banged up at Her Majesty's pleasure and I feel sorry for them. One of these characters is quite infamous. I have never met him but I did see him once at Caulfield. This was before he got into the tight situation that he is now in: Barwon Prison.

The sighting was in the birdcage area. He was carrying a bag of hydroponic carrots and petting a horse in one of the corner stalls. I couldn't help but think that anyone who likes animals can't be all that bad. Naturally, I checked out the form of the horse that had taken his fancy. It was inglorious, to say the least. Two hours later, the same colt spread-eagled a class field to win a premium race by eight lengths. It was then that I started to look at organic vegetables in a new light.

Not many horses can run one thousand meters in fifty-six seconds. The important thing is that they think they can. That's what it's about. Confidence! In the past, I have been a great believer in motivation but now I will have to seriously look at a horse's diet, when considering my investments. On reflection, all my best tips have come from Ron the fruitologist, although his asparagus was usually rubbish.

In truth, I rarely win my battles with bookmakers. However, there are some who do. The professional gambler is easy to spot at the track. He's the cool dude with the confident look on his face. Need I mention that he will be sporting an Armani suit with a club tie and shades? The club tie is fraudulent and the sunnies are there to hide the terror in his eyes. He will be transfixed to the same spot for most of the day and will nod at passing acquaintances and fellow optimists. Occasionally, he does move and if you were to follow him, you would get to see the mounting yard, the Birdcage, the tote hall and the Champagne Bar. Strangely, he will only make one visit to the main betting ring.

During the last week, he has chalked up twenty-two hours of computer time, watched thirty-six hours of video replays, attended sixteen horse trials, flipped through reams of statistical information and is familiar with weather patterns in all states and territories. After all that, he makes just one bet.

The average punter has little time for assessment and no time at all for reflection. There will be another race, somewhere in Australia, within two minutes of the last. Enter the form analysts, racing journalists and tipping services. With these people around, you need know nothing. It is only after you realize that they know nothing that the penny drops. Last week's pay should have been channeled into food, rent and other essential items. If your wife finds that IOU in the kiddies' piggy bank you are in big trouble.

There is always the possibility that you could send the little woman along to Flemington in your place. Novice gamblers have this unbelievable skill of winning first up. Such success, following on from your failure, would be a jolt to your pride but you can be smug in the knowledge that there is now another passenger aboard the last train to heartbreak hill.

Cadet punters start to salivate as soon as they receive their first dividend. Rational thought goes out the window and soon she will be asking someone where you can buy a season ticket. Once caressed by the god of greed, you haven't got a prayer. Excited expectation is replaced by disgust and despondency. Desperate Housewife syndrome may kick in if she shortens her name from Betty to Bet. The other downside will occur when the twins mature to manhood. There will probably be no venture capital available for that pig farm that you've always wanted for them.

Some wives will not be so compliant and it may be necessary for you to operate as an off-course punter. You will be available for domestic chores and that is probably an acceptable compromise. Television and radio bring every exciting moment into your own domain and you don't miss a thing. Unfortunately, you may have to listen to whining media commentators, who will tell you that you are all hard done-by, due to the lack of transparency in racing. If you've got a clear picture in the den, a bar fridge and a pool table, you're not hard done-by, at all. For the wife's benefit, you can patch through to the kitchen, your new CD of international lawn mower sounds. If she wises up to that one and sends you shopping, that's even better. There's always a PubTAB on the way.

The Spring Carnival!

When I first met the lovely Leanne, my heart skipped a beat. She was attractive, talented and socially popular. So much so, that my overtures were rejected out of hand. A glutton for punishment, I persisted but with little joy. I was therefore surprised when she rang me and said *I want to go to the races*. Yes, I was the holder of a prized guest ticket for you know where and you don't have to be a salacious ogre to salivate over the leverage that this can give you with the fairer sex. But enough about me.

Last year was her first appearance at the Melbourne Spring Racing Carnival and now she says she wouldn't miss it for the world. I have to admit that she did look stunning in her outlandishly oversized hat, which contrasted brilliantly with her daring mini skirt. I was justifiably proud and she was quietly smug. I only hoped that her presence didn't prove a distraction to the real job at hand — picking winners.

Yours truly is conversant with every nook and cranny of all our celebrated racing venues, so the lady couldn't have had a better guide. We started with the engine room — the Bookmaker's Ring. My mother always advised me to stay away from men with shoulder bags but these people are the essence of the racing game. Tales are forever told of gargantuan betting duels and controversial characters. I could tell that Leanne was hooked and she didn't need much encouragement to participate in this thrilling form of financial investment — except that she didn't bring any money. I don't have to tell you where she got it from and I didn't expect her to keep it.

Lunch is always a good idea, if you're going to make a big day of it. She insisted that we acquire a table that wasn't too far away from a betting opportunity and I assured her that this was entirely possible. Tote windows are conveniently placed throughout the course, in the dining rooms and near the train station, just in case patrons have ideas of leaving the track with some readies in their pocket or purse.

During our meal, I was able to elaborate on some of this sport's most defining moments and where else could magical memories be better promulgated than in this elegant oak-paneled haven of hospitality? History was dripping from the wall hangings as all of those champions from the past gazed down on us benevolently. Unfortunately, she was only half listening. Someone had placed the smorgasbord near the betting convenience and isn't a journey of delight always enhanced with a detour? Our table appeared to be growing tote tickets and her good ear was forever cocked to the imminent prospect of another broadcast from Rosehill, Morphettville, Doomben or Deniliquin.

I always like to take a walk after dining and usually suggest a visit to the Birdcage. This is where they keep the animals prior to their appointment with destiny. It's good to take a bird to the Birdcage. However, here is one tip, girls. Don't stand too close to the horseflesh. Just prior to the Victoria Derby, one of the horses left a large legacy on lissome Leanne's legs, as he lightened his load for the long race.

Did I mention that Flemington is a bit of a fashion battleground? My consort had eyes in the back of her head but fortunately there was no duplicate outfit and her hat remained a curious tribute to geometric insanity. For the purists, Derby Day is without equal. It is also the first day that the couturiers and milliners unleash their creations on the assembled throng — usually with devastating effect.

A Gorilla is a one thousand dollar wager. You may also be standing next to one at the payout window on Cup Day. Yes, fancy dress is the choice of many but the Oaks Day meeting is when the gloves are off. I find that honest comment on these matters of fashion and sartorial elegance is fraught with danger. To avoid being harpooned in a sea of doubt, I try and get away from the catwalk as quickly as possible. An invitation to the Champagne Bar is rarely rejected or one could consider the actual races, which are preceded by traditional preliminaries. Any self-respecting analyst will want to inspect the thoroughbreds in the mounting yard.

There would be few animals that are not trained to the minute and this will be self-evident when you consider their coat, confirmation and mental stability. With considerable fanfare, the jocks are announced, instructed and lifted aboard. They will pray for a perfect passage into posterity and so will you.

Adrenalin is a funny thing. It kicks in just after anticipation and only eases off after a gratuitous round of drinks at the bar. Sometimes, it returns when you discover that you've selected the right number in the wrong race. If you are unaware of the vagaries of racing patterns, track conditions, weight-for-age, apprentice claims, sectionals, winkers and blinkers, you will only be interested in the latter stages of any given race. Certainly, this was when Leanne first realized that she was a live chance. Her screams were worthy of an Alfred Hitchcock masterpiece. Sadly, she lost in a photo but what the heck — it was only my money.

-5-

TRAVEL

The people across the water

California Getaway

The other side of the world

Sand in my shoes

Some people look at frequent travelers with great envy and never tire of dropping by to see your photographic memories. Then there is the majority of the population. Other people's journeys are as exciting as a kiss from your mother-in-law.

My escapades have been depreciated by time and enhanced by exaggeration so I can only be vague about the extent of their accuracy. I have chosen to highlight my adventures in places where there are no outstanding warrants pending. This allows me to be both forthright and honest. Well, forthright, anyway.

THE PEOPLE ACROSS THE WATER

If you reside in Western Australia, you live in a state of excitement. I'm from Victoria. We are cool, calm and collected and always subdued in our enthusiasm for anything. If you factor in the fact that my destination, this day, was to be New Zealand, you can understand why I was asleep before the cab had made it to the airport.

I was once told that you should never look a Kiwi in the eye. Somehow they know that you are not one of them. Even before you open your mouth, they will recognize you for what you are: a no-good slime-bucket who has under-arm problems, even if you smell nice. That infamous under-arm cricket episode created an international incident that permanently damaged relationships across the Ditch (Tasman Sea). New Zealanders love to see you arrive on the back foot and I checked to see that I didn't have "All Australians are cheats" stamped on my passport.

I was bound for Queenstown, the jewel in the crown of the south island. Victoria was named after our mother country's most auspicious monarch, as was Queenstown, so you would figure that there might be some affinity with the locals. First of all, you have to find some locals. Leading the tourist charge was Bill Gates, private plane and all. The rest of us had to take the airplane with propellers. How quaint. The passengers were aghast and agog as the pilot maneuvered his way through the snow-capped peaks and then dumped us at our destination. Bill must have seen us coming. I was told that the Microsoft man had elected to take the hard drive to Blanket Bay. There was so much that I wanted to say to him.

I was soon entrenched in my comfortable digs overlooking the often photographed Lake Wakatipu, which is admirably translucent but a little chilly. When I travel, I always like to take the waters. Here, hyperthermia sets in after ten minutes and if time gets away from you, one might just drop into the unknown depths. Another useless Aussie, down where he belongs. I enjoyed a wonderful nine minute swim and hurried back to base before the relatives could start searching for the will.

Somebody was talking-up the scenic gondola ride to the peak, overlooking the underlying district. However, the picture book setting was on the other side of the lake: The Remarkables. I don't usually applaud understatement but whoever named this magnificent mountain range erred on the side of conservatism. The early settlers were mostly Scots and you don't have to be impressed that I know this. There's another mountain on the island which is called Ben Nevis. The highest peak in Britain would be just a pimple in this environment but I guess if you are homesick, why not indulge in a little geographic plagiarism.

Like many of you, I get hungry when I am on holidays. There were about sixty restaurants to investigate and the menu in one window already had my attention. They promised to whet the appetite, amuse my mouth and invigorate my palate. The food was good and the waiters were able to be understood. New Zealanders speak a hybrid version of English and in Central Otago, intersperse it with cute Scottish idioms like "wee" and "dram."

These are hospitable people and they will offer you a glass of wine pre-lunch, during lunch and post-lunch. They will then suggest a winery tour which includes an afternoon tasting and an evening listening to music amongst the vines. Their product is excellent and you can repeat this regime every day of your two week vacation and never walk on familiar ground. I was certainly up for it and book-ended the magic meals with a game of golf and a visit to the Casino. If you don't like wine, brewery tours are also available but Australians should be prepared for the almost predictable insult.

If you are so inclined, you can lug your golf clubs around to all the courses in the area. There are about half a dozen different layouts and none so pretty as the Kelvin Heights landscape that juts out into the deep blue waters of the lake. You'll need a car to visit Arrowtown, a delightful and picturesque old mining settlement and a must visit destination. Along the way, you will see people jumping off bridges, hurtling though space, riding the rapids and attempting other death-defying pursuits. New Zealand is the home of adventure tourism.

This is where it's at if you want to terminate yourself. Bungy jumping, jet-boat riding, white-water rafting and skydiving are all portals to the after-life. Go on. Defy gravity and live to tell the tale. The backpackers are lined up en masse because these kids want a rush but I'm not in so much of a hurry. Being a Sunday driver kind of person, I chose the scenic trail along Skippers Gorge. I should have known better. That entry kiosk sold nothing but rosary beads.

After you pass the sign that says that you are no longer insured, you freewheel along a narrow, one lane, gravel track that descends sharply along a terrifying-looking precipice. It is all downhill until you get to Hell's Gates. If you can find a turning point, take it. The way back is marginally easier on the nerves but next time, I would definitely do it before I visited the winery.

If you have blood pressure problems, a weak heart, high anxiety or dropsy, the Kiwis aren't particularly interested. If you depart this mortal coil on their patch, they will be disappointed but take the attitude that one less Australian can't be such a bad thing. Take a walk on the wild side if you must but there are many alternatives. You can trek or cycle through the mountains or amble through a flat beech forest. Milford Sound also beckons; so do the other southern lakes and glaciers. Autumn and spring create their own delights. In winter you can ski.

If you thought that this might be the land that time forgot, you are mistaken. It is unforgettable as a holiday destination and those who have visited will have tall tales and fond memories. The Lord of the Rings was nearby. In fact, he may still be. Jennifer Aniston didn't want to leave, or Bill Clinton. I expect he was there for the fly fishing.

Ride it like you've stolen it.

When I was a little fella, this stranger said that he would walk a million miles for one of my smiles. Or did he sing it? Obviously, I was too young to recognize a pedophile in action and accepted his assessment of my magnetism as legitimate. For ten years I became quite confident in my ability to charm and beguile members of both sexes, although, on reflection, most were favorite aunts and uncles or other close family members. It all went terribly wrong when I presented myself for my first dance at the Heidelberg Town Hall. I couldn't get a walk up start with Ugly Betty. The man from Colgate Palmolive had just laid an egg.

I think that this is when I first decided that horses were less complicated creatures than women and I decided to give them my complete and total concentration. People who know me realize that I would walk a million miles to attend a race meeting. That's how I ended up in the ass end of New Zealand in a small settlement named Glenorchy.

It is fair to say that the picnic meeting at Glenorchy is like no other. For a start, the events are held on the local golf course and in true entrepreneurial style: the organizers always retain one of the putting greens for a hole-in-one competition. A further fairway was being used for a cricket competition, which required you to bowl out an Aussie, underarm. I was more interested in the horse flesh and of course, the betting ring. If I could recoup some of my outgoings that I had squandered at the various wineries in the area, this would be good. It would also allow for more squandering. They then hit me with their Sunday punch. There was no betting ring — only a tote which they called the Equilisator, where you could not bet on your chosen horse. You received a ticket indicating a letter of the alphabet and the name of your runner was announced just prior to starter's orders. These are crazy people.

I have attended many thoroughbred meetings and I know that stewards are never generous in their appreciation of team riding, as a concept. This was all about team riding. A small group of teenage nymphets were clustered together, trying to map out their strategy for the day's events. They were togged up in matching tee shirts, with motivational artistry boldly emblazoned across their ample bosoms: *Ride it like you've stolen it.*

I was under cover near the second turn and nuzzling on a delicate Otago pinot noir, when the field for the first race thundered by. It took some time before my representative presented himself but there he was, proudly displaying number forty-seven on his rump. I was hoping that the jockette was a good judge of pace and that the animal would take closer orders the second time around. Not to be. This was a horse that nobody would want to steal and the dividend was paid elsewhere: a whopping seven dollars.

The next five races also paid seven dollars and then we came to the main event of the day. I was on the favorite and had every reason to be confident. The horse in question, a ten year old Clydesdale, was a legend in the area and had distinguished himself on five previous occasions. In stature, he towered above the rest and as there appeared to be no handicap conditions, I could not see him being beaten. Of course, being a city slicker and a first-time visitor to this neck of the woods, you would have to think that it was never going to be as simple as that. Did Rose Kennedy own a black dress?

It turns out that I was on the crowd favorite, not the tote favorite and it appears that there was a handicapping system as perverse as any that I have ever seen on a race track. Albeit unsophisticated, it was practical and had the desired effect. Unfortunately, the novice punters were all unaware of what was to unfold. For the first part of the journey the race was up for grabs and my charger was doing me proud. Then, to my horror, the horses all stopped, turned around and started to take on passengers. Horror upon horror, the poor Clydesdale had to take on not one but two extra riders and naturally slipped back through the field, as he lumbered to the line. Nevertheless, he received the largest ovation and the winning dividend was seven dollars. One of the winning jockeys was a tourist from Glasgow.

I decided to retire my investments and we all settled down with a few more bottles of vino and marveled at the panoramic surroundings. It was just as well. The last race only had three starters and the winning dividend was two dollars.

One can never be content with just one race meeting, while on holidays, so a visit to the Omakau picnic races was also in my itinerary, hail, rain or shine. Here, they boasted real bookmakers and they love Aussie money. However, the horses, in their inimitable fashion, treated me with distain. I will not bore you with the details but I have recently been nominated into the Psychic's Hall of Fame and you have to ask the question. "Why, then, can I never pick a winner?"

I don't think my nag is going to catch up.

Always on the money!

I attended school with the son of an American wrestler called Chief Little Wolf. He was the most inquisitive kid I ever knew and forever questioning our science teacher. He always used to raise his hand and say *How*. I refer to this long cherished memory because I think that there is a great similarity between the American Indian and the indigenous New Zealander. The Māori is fierce, aggressive and heavily into body decoration. So is Mrs Māori. This is the home of Xena — Warrior Princess.

We are talking about a proud sporting nation, although I do think that the people are sometimes a bit confused. Some ethnic groups are color sensitive and prefer to call themselves Afro-Americans. New Zealand sporting teams identify themselves as All Blacks, Tall Blacks, Iron Blacks, Ice Blacks, Black Caps, Black Sox, Black Sticks and Black Ferns and, for a short while, the Badminton team was the Black Cocks. Yet, they are coffee colored at worst. However, don't call them Small Blacks. They get offended easily.

The Kiwis are great achievers. They beat the United States in the America's Cup and mostly everyone at rugby. Their racehorses have even won the Melbourne Cup. Nevertheless, all these triumphs are insignificant when you consider the achievements of their women. A few years ago, theirs was the only country in the world in which the highest offices in the land were occupied simultaneously by women: from the Queen (titular head) through to the Governor General, Prime Minister, Chief Justice and the Speaker of the House of Representatives. I won't comment on this any further because I just know that I will put my foot in it.

I always try and meet a lot of women when I am traveling and I am fast overcoming my allergy to mace. However, you don't really get to meet many local Kiwis until you're on the plane out of there. In Australia, we have a very generous social service system and we like to feed and clothe the disadvantaged, no matter where they come from. The unemployment office at Bondi Beach is one of the largest reunion points for New Zealanders in our country. Life is difficult in this financial environment and this largely agricultural country is renowned for living off the sheep's back. I should mention that this is a colloquial expression and in no way infers an intimate relationship.

The land of the long white cloud is an English interpretation of the Māori description of the place whilst the name New Zealand owes its roots to Dutch settlers and has no connection to Old Zealand, which is Danish. I don't really want to give you a history lesson but you need to know these things because the time will come when you will need ammunition to rebuff insults and the like. Every time I step down from my aircraft at Heathrow, there is some small-minded individual who wants to remind me that my forebears were convicts. I am dying for the day when I can whip out a Saturday night special and declare that I am still on the lam.

All holidays must end and so must this dispatch. I hope that my passport will not be shredded by ungrateful bureaucrats and that I can once again visit this spectacular tourist destination. If you appreciate clean air, mighty vistas and exciting challenges, such a trip might even be worthy for your next adventure. Just don't mention my name before they lock you in for your bungy jump.

I hope I haven't offended him.

CALIFORNIA GETAWAY

Mojave is in the desert. If you really wanted to go there, you would pass a mausoleum of decomposing jumbo jets, a tragic and forlorn sight, even for someone like me. My fear of flying has me forever labeled as a coward of coach class. The ribbon of highway eventually arrived at some kind of excuse for civilization. The tumbling tumbleweeds gamboled provocatively around the perimeter of my wheels and the morning gave up a ghostly silence, in anticipation of yet another uncomfortable day of high temperatures. This would be a town without pity.

In actuality, it was only half a town. There was only one side to the main street. The railway line ran along the other boundary and whichever way you looked at it, the town was built on the wrong side of the tracks. From the open doorway of an air-conditioned Denny's franchise, I heard Boxcar Willie belting out an old Hank Williams favorite. They were doing breakfast for $2.99 so I went in.

I can hear you gasp from here. As sure as Pope Benedict likes eggs, where do you get breakfast for that kind of money? OK, you've got me there. This is an old story but it has to be. If you appreciate the culture of intelligence organizations, you will understand that there is a statute of limitations on information and unless you can get it out through a dead letter drop or a cipher exchange, it must hibernate in the cobwebs of time. Certain people may still treat me with extreme prejudice when they hear what I have to say and that is why, when you have read my narrative, please tear out the pages and eat them.

There was a new boy in town. As I slowly masticated on my morning meal, the locals were eyeballing me with all their steely determination. Hadn't they ever seen a redneck before? I suppose I shouldn't have ordered the Earl Grey with the breakfast Burrito. It was a dead giveaway. Then again, half the red-blooded males in this neck of the woods were called Earl; so where's the side-show? I have road-tested many diners in God's own country and they are quite unique. Nevertheless, I have never really warmed to flapjacks, grits, hash browns and chili dogs, all washed down with copious cups of caffeine. The powdered creamer is optional but the tip isn't. The waitress will call you Honey but her smile quickly dissipates when you tell her that you are committed to Kellogg's.

Once their curiosity was appeased, I was able to ruminate on my forthcoming meeting with Cal. He was due at any moment. Of course, spies don't often clock-on when they should and I was left waiting for two and a half hours. What a shame they didn't have cell phones in those days. Evidently, he was holed up in a nearby town with a lady of the night. Lone Pine is a nondescript little whistle stop with a large Indian presence and they milk it for all it is worth. When I passed through, I noticed Gene Autrey Drive, Tom Mix Street and Hopalong Cassidy Avenue. I lunched at the John Wayne Restaurant. They were advertising the best hamburgers in town. It was one of the worst hamburgers that I have ever eaten.

Five miles away, the gulches and canyons had been a mandatory location for every Western movie that was ever made but now they are living on memories. The last chaps to be seen in this territory were part of the Cottontails tour. Today, it would be difficult to keep the jet streams out of shot, not that they make cowboy films any more. I did see a Greyhound bus slide by, which reminded me that they can also be a director's nightmare. You may recall one such vehicle appearing in the background of the Roman epic *Ben Hur*.

Back in Mojave, I was trying to work out why Cal chose such a place for a rendezvous. After reading the map, it became clear. We were only thirty minutes from Edwards Air Force Base and the weapons testing area was further up the road. Still, he would have to be careful to protect his anonymity. Recently, my partner had been the much celebrated centerfold for *Spy Monthly* and his style and procedures were well recognized. Fortunately, he was a master of disguise.

Cal arrived wearing a yellow and pink Hawaiian shirt, cargo pants, moccasins, shades and a Mexican Sombrero. You might say that he snuck into town. The job was as challenging as any that had gone before and I was his wing man. Naturally, I can't tell you anything about our mission but it did concern one of the aforementioned installations. He even had an escape plan which initially encouraged me. Graduates from the Maxwell Smart School of Espionage don't usually look that far ahead.

I don't know why I had misgivings. The instructions were quite simple. Take Route 66 until you are just twenty-four hours from Tulsa. By the time you get to Phoenix, it will be Kansas City, here I come. It occurred to me that his daughter worked for a record company and I wondered if she had devised the escape plan.

In the end, we escaped and it was every man for himself. I headed north and eventually found myself hitch-hiking in the eerie half-light of evening in a redwood forest. The trees were so tall they almost touched the moon and the shadows were lengthening by the minute. I thought that darkness would be my friend until I remembered that I was afraid of the dark. By the roadside, the bushes started rustling and the howling commenced. Although I couldn't read my watch, I knew it was dinner time. Their dinner time! I was giving off a smell of fear and trepidation and my deodorant definitely wasn't working.

Salvation finally arrived in the form of a sleek convertible, driven by a cool cowboy who was obviously a fashion plate in his own world. From the manner of his hair grooming, I deduced that he was from one of the oil-rich states, perhaps Texas. I had not been in the country long enough to appreciate the vagaries of the vernacular but as he talked with a toothpick protruding from his mouth, I assumed that he was not a Harvard graduate.

There is something about the comfort of strangers. If you are female or pubescent, new friends should be approached with caution but for those of us who are unattractive and oblivious to danger, there is nothing better than a four hour horror ride in a super-charged gas guzzler, on the road to nowhere with a certified maniac. Being a foreigner is always helpful in situations like this because you can become an ambassador for your country and everything will be a revelation to the average West Coast nomad. On the other side of the country, the New York cabby is far more opinionated. One is required to have no conversation but a ready ear to listen to the world's foremost authority on just about everything.

Most of us talk about subjects that we are familiar with: home, work, football and more football. It was no different with my driver except that his line of work was running drugs. His trunk was full of the stuff and I can only presume that the highway patrol were reticent to lift the lid in case they found a dead body. At various times during our road trip, I thought it might be me. Spy school had not prepared me for this. Sure, I could be devious, deceitful, innocuous and insignificant but the truth of the matter was that I was a hundred and fifty pound weakling. If this guy sat on me, I was toast.

Tex had some legitimate student friends who were polite, charming and relatively conservative. They were obviously customers and also a hitching post on the periodical drug run. I was invited to stay overnight, if I didn't mind sleeping on the sofa, beneath what I thought was the fish tank. Somehow, the python woke me from my slumber and although the snake was under glass, it turned out to be a restless night.

Nevertheless, I enjoyed the stopover because there was a lot happening in this part of America. People were talking about a rupture in the San Andreas Fault and some motor homes in Washington had experienced a lava shower from the Mount St Helen's volcano. I decided that it was time to move on and under my own steam. I was able to purchase commemorative souvenirs of these events on the way out. The secret to good marketing is to move quickly.

The sight of the Golden Gate Bridge brought back many memories: when people had flowers in their hair and a silly grin on their face. Hallucinatory drugs will do that to you. I collected my meager belongings, bid farewell to the Amtrak flyer and headed for the left luggage office. People often leave things behind in San Francisco and for our agency, this was standard operating procedure. I collected our standard travel package from the third member of our team. She was masquerading as a baggage attendant. It contained a Beretta automatic with three rounds of ammunition and a Brazilian passport in the name of Schnook Gomez. There were also two front row tickets to a Bette Midler concert. This was the extra bonus that you got if your operations supervisor was gay.

Sadly, I noticed Dirty Harry's Magnum revolver gathering dust in a corner compartment and Tony Bennett's heart was still there. Shouldn't these things be in a museum or something? Of course, Harry was no longer in the law enforcement business and was running a restaurant franchise in Carmel. Somehow, he had managed to convince the local peasants to elect him mayor. When I heard this, it made my day.

They had put a moustache on my mug-shot but there was no way that I was going to look Brazilian until I could get myself a tan. I belted the Beretta, rented an SUV and headed off to the Big Sur. San Francisco is a wonderful place to disappear. That's why they have so many magicians' conventions there. The Big Sur is something else. Perfect panoramas and magnificent vistas will compliment your drive along a freeway that straddles the Pacific Coast between 'Frisco and Los Angeles. But the area is so much more than just the topography of dramatic cliff faces, smashing surf and golden beaches.

The American ethos is accentuated by real places that are perpetuated by events, historical memory and time-honored folklore. While Hollywood superstars were filming scary movies out of Carmel, the jazz people were making history at Monterey and inland, the ghost of Steinbeck was alive and well in Salinas. The Grapes of Wrath are no more but the oranges are still juicy and succulent.

I gunned my little road rodent as much as I could. I was off to meet one of those Hollywood superstars. The air was fresh and the Californian sun was being as kind as possible. On the radio, the local DJ was introducing somebody called Bar-Bar-Barbara Ann. The Beach Boys had stormed into the charts with a bullet. Didn't I tell you that this was an old story?

When I arrived in Carmel, the afternoon sun was starting to wane and it was Happy Hour at the Hog's Breath Inn. There were five Harley-Davidsons parked outside the entrance. Home is where the heart is. Inside, the Easy Riders were all at the bar but I gave them a wide berth. Wasn't it Oscar Wilde who said: *Hell hath no fury like an Angel on a motor bike?* Perhaps it was Oscar Madison. I went straight through to the kitchen and found Clint in front of a crock of soup. He had a ladle in one hand and a movie script in the other. He wanted me to sample the broth: *Hey, punk. Are you feeling lucky?*

I was terrified and nearly dropped my autograph book. *Y-y-yes, Mr Eastwood*, I stammered but I was far from enthusiastic. It was ox-tail soup alright but I think it might have been underdone. There appeared to be three tails trying to escape over the rim. In the end, Clint was the first to admit that he wasn't cut out to be a chef and passed the reins to someone who was eminently qualified. The franchise blossomed and he lived off the earnings. I used to have a distant relative like that. I think he had something like twelve daughters.

Clint was kind enough to treat me to a Boss Hog Double Burger for the road and I appreciated that. He said that I was the nicest Brazilian that he had ever met. I was loath to ask him how many South Americans he knew but I am sure that some of them might have been gangsters. It was good to know that the disguise was actually working but I could never be sure until I had tested it before a Latino scrutineer. So, I headed south to try and find one of those Cantinas that are prevalent around the LA area.

My first Margarita was easy to take; not so the noise in the background. The Tex/Mex band sounded like Freddy Fender with road rage. Where was Linda Ronstadt when I needed her? Overall, the Mexicans were very friendly people and none of them found it suspicious that I was a Brazilian who couldn't speak Portuguese. Many had crossed the border on numerous occasions and their geographical knowledge proved invaluable when assessing my options on how to escape from America. I suppose I could have caught a plane but why spoil a good story?

The train ride from Mexicali to Mazatlan was one of the most harrowing that I have known. If you are contemplating such a journey, I suggest a commando course would be a suitable preparation. They sell every seat three times and you will need a few knee-jerks and a Karate chop in order to secure your place. The train is air-conditioned, due to the fact that all the windows remain open, which is necessary because at every station, enchiladas, hot tamales and other highly suspect food items are thrust at the starving passengers. Some of them hadn't eaten since the last stop.

This was the first time that I had spent twenty-four hours in cattle class and on arrival my relief was obvious. My first espionage job was over and it was a great success. Australia would now have the resources and capability to bomb New Zealand. The Prime Minister was ecstatic.

THE OTHER SIDE OF THE WORLD

I had just farted. My fellow travelers in the arrivals queue scrambled sideways in search of clean air and I realized how Moses must have felt when he parted the Red Sea. I suspect that I moved much more quickly. From my rear position, I immediately propelled myself forward to obtain a more prominent place in the line. I was only seconds away from receiving a warm and glorious welcome to the land of hope and glory. Or so I thought.

This was my first visit to Britain. I was following a long and worn path, many times trodden by Australians since my granny was in diapers. Usually, one would make the journey at some time between graduation and legitimate employment but I had been working for several years: first, as an accountant and then my years in advertising. I also spent time in the secret service but I can't talk about that. Already a seasoned traveler, one had access to a number of passports. For some reason, I decided to be Irish. This was a bad choice.

The lass at the customs and immigration counter didn't appear to have a sense of humor. For years, my dynamic personality and charming disposition had made me a favorite with the chicky-babes right across the country. However, all that I could see was a brutal and scornful disregard for my playful antipodean wit. To be fair, there was a bit of tension in the air. The IRA had been very busy of late and only in the last few days, a nasty bomb had taken out a number of people in Belgium. To my complete surprise, they asked me to step aside and I was separated from my passport for thirty-five minutes.

I suppose that it was rather ironic that I should come under scrutiny in this way because my own father was a member of the IRA when they wore uniforms. I don't know how many skirmishes he had with the *Black and Tans* but I do know that the English were not his favorite people. Finally, my passport was returned and I was allowed to continue my journey. On the way out I passed a large *Wanted* poster of the bomb suspect. He was the spitting image of me.

What can I tell you about the U.K. that you don't already know? It is indeed a land of contrasts: beauty and squalor, pomp and circumstance, rich and poor. Some two hundred years earlier, our forebears were etching out a living as robbers, murderers and general villains, convicts all. I don't think they will ever let us forget it. Of course, we ended up with a Pacific paradise, a vibrant economy and a population that looks good in bikinis and budgie smugglers.

I don't know where I went wrong but it was three hours before I met another English person. This was an ethnic melting pot. A camel train of Rolls Royce vehicles passed me by. From inside I picked up these strange incantations to Allah. Being a bit peckish, I wanted to try a typical British meal. I was told that this would be curry. So much for the pie and mushy peas that I had heard so much about. I found digs in a predictable part of town which was well served with Fosters Lager, lots of sheilas and cheap kebabs. You've got to start somewhere. In the end, I found myself an English job, an English girl-friend and moved to an English part of town. I couldn't complain. I shared an apartment with two gorgeous models and the flat was above a Ladbroke's Betting Shop with a pub right next door. I was earning good money so I bought myself a BMW. My miserable work-mates absolutely hated that.

A lot of people in my country are Republicans but there would be few who don't respect the monarch, if not the monarchy. I am quite indifferent to this whole independence thing but I can see that it will gather impetus if the young royals start to lose their popularity. You can tell when they are on the nose if people wave at them but they're not using all their fingers.

Their mother was a real sweetie. I remember Lady Diana with great affection and used to see a lot of her when she worked out at her gym, every week. Of course, some times the binoculars fogged up when the weather rolled in but what can you do about that? England can be a gloomy place.

The intemperate English weather interrupts the cricket, the tennis, the Ascot Gold Cup and the festivities at Henley-on-Thames. The Brits remain stoic through it all. Stiff upper lip, old chap. There might be sunshine through the gloom if a downpour coincides with a batting collapse at Lords because the locals rarely win. A lanky Scot is their only chance to be in a Wimbledon final for over seventy years and most of their horse races are won by a Sheik of Araby or the Aga Khan. It's enough to make you want to immigrate to Australia.

Actually, one of my contemporaries contemplated such a move. They offered him big money but he couldn't bring himself to leave his bed-sit in Barnes. He was comfortable in his own world which was a pub that served warm beer and soggy chips. Admittedly, it did have a pool table and dart board.

I didn't have the heart to mention our jelly wrestling and topless bar-maids. Not that this would have interested him. He was gay. In fact, I think that his life partner was instrumental in the desire to stay put. The sod had sensitive skin and the harsh Australian sun would have been destructive. Although Rob did tell me that he found compromising photos under their bed — of life-savers, no less.

Being from convict stock, one of the skills that you quickly learn is the art of deception and I was able to put this to good use in my early days in the Old Dart — long before the beautiful models and the BMW. Although I used to dress like a finance director, my main source of income was sales turnover from the cars and vans that I used to nick around the Australia House area. It wasn't really stealing. Most had been abandoned by the comrades after their European sojourn and I could sell them with a two day money back guarantee. Of course, I was long gone after two hours.

This is when I met Valerie: at a meet and greet soiree for likely lads and upwardly mobile fornicators. I was unaware that she was aware of my sordid occupation. I thought that she was particularly attractive and told her so. She was relatively compliant and I believed that she imagined that I was a person of substance, which I wasn't.

In a polite and pleasant manner, I told her that she was charming and personable and acknowledged that I had been advised of her impressive qualifications, although I had no idea what they were. Before the conversation was over, I had offered her a job as chair of a new bio-tech company that I was putting together. There was no such company. These are the things I do to try and impress people. We swapped business cards and parted company.

I don't know who told her about my commercial endeavors but I think she rather liked people with a bit of form. Whenever there was a bank robbery or some other scurrilous activity on the front page of the tabloids, she would ring and ask whether I had anything to do with it. She was certainly one of a kind. The word on the street was that the lady was related to people in high places in the Philippines and I could believe that. She had an awful lot of shoes.

Valerie: Getting ready to kick ass.

These street people are an unsavory lot and it was through one of these meatheads that I discovered that Valerie was not all that she seemed. It came as a great shock to me to eventually learn that she was working front-of-house at a notorious Soho establishment, where the men were men but the women were carrying extra baggage.

I didn't know what to think but surely she would understand that the bio-tech job was no longer on the table. My worst fears were realized when she asked if I would drive her to the clinic for her sex change operation. I did that but it was all too much for me. I just kept going. Intrepid travelers know that you can stay in one place for too long and so a trip to the Continent wasn't such a bad idea. I had long cherished the desire to visit every racecourse in the world and the Froggies had some good horse flesh.

If you are lucky, you can get overnight accommodation in Paris but the rack rate is about the equivalent of the Lindbergh ransom demand. I discovered a cool loft on the fourth floor of a Left Bank relic but you needed two trips to transport all your baggage. The hit and run robbers only needed one trip to ransack my car of everything valuable but the rogues were discerning thieves. They had unzipped my suit bag and left behind anything that didn't have a designer label. I can understand the fastidious nature of their trade because up-market apparel in France is without equal. You can end up looking a million dollars and it will only cost you half of that.

The city of light has long been a lure for lovers. A walk along the banks of the Seine is nothing if not romantic and the plaintive overlay of a melodic Maurice Chevalier supplication will melt the most prosaic heart. In truth, I am more of an Edith Piaf kind of person. She was so wonderfully depressing and the origins of her road to glory were the sad streets of Montmartre and Montparnasse, seductively situated on either side of the river. In those days, loving was cheap in this part of town and so were the room rentals. The area became a magnet for the artistic community and their bohemian existence stimulated and excited the general population. Many lived in communes and at various stages attracted the likes of Dalí, Monet, Picasso and Van Gogh. It was a tough life. Jean Cocteau famously declared: *Poverty is a luxury in Montparnasse.*

The area was even inhabited by those popular foreign exiles Lenin and Trotsky and a whole heap of writers such as Beckett, Henry Miller, James Joyce, Hemingway and F. Scott Fitzgerald. Now we are in my area of expertise. I reckon that they were there for the high jinks that went on at the Moulin Rouge and La Chat Noir. These types of establishments still exist but only some of them retain their original format. You can close your eyes and dream of a Josephine Baker spectacular but as soon as you open them, you realize that you are outside a peep show in Pigalle.

An art lover can be spoiled for choice in Paris. I didn't know whether to spend a lazy afternoon at the Louvre or head off to the track for some exciting thoroughbred action. When I saw that the favorite for the main race was five to two in the morning line, it became a no-brainer. On the way, I picked up some postcards of the Mona Lisa and other desirables. It was the perfect compromise.

I made eight bad decisions at Longchamp and the next one would be the most important. How to scamper from my hotel without paying the bill! That drain pipe from the fourth floor looked really wonky.

In the end, I left just before dawn and didn't look back until the car broke down in the middle of who knows where. The provincial countryside can be so pretty. You only have to watch the Tour de France on the telly to know that. Unfortunately, my surrounds were a stark reminder that they only put the nice bits on the television. The place was devoid of friendly helpful people and the road service took forever to come to my rescue. This may well have been due to the fact that I told them that I had broken down on the outskirts of a town called Ralentissez. It appears that this is the French word to slow down.

Why would you have to urge country folk to slow down? It's part of their nature. In fact, I have purchased a number of racehorses from the country and they have been very slow. Although I was keen to make up lost time, the local gas station was closed for lunch and such a meal usually takes two or three hours in this neck of the woods. What could I do but embrace their traditional rituals? I'm glad I did. The *Boeuf Provencale* was superb and tasted just like my Aunty Pat's Saturday stew. The local wine was more than acceptable and the after-dinner nap was just what I needed; after all, I had been up since dawn.

You can always smell port towns a long time before you see them. Marseille was no different. The aroma of rotting bollards and putrid seaweed is something that immediately challenges the most traveled of snouts. People tell me that I have a nose for trouble and I immediately knew that I should keep away from the waterfront. Then somebody told me about the Bouillabaisse: a fish dish to die for. A different somebody told me that the murder rate in Marseille was ten times the average and that I should always eat with my back to the wall. This was good advice and with a great deal of bravado and some anxiety, I ravaged the soup with relish. If I did sustain a nasty injury, there were plenty of drugs in town to hasten my recovery.

My next stop was Monte Carlo, home to the Grimaldi clan, assorted tax evaders, formula one devotees and a magnificent casino. I have always felt disposed to try and include a casino visit into my itinerary and this one is priceless. There is something perversely satisfying about losing your money under a gigantic chandelier that may have reflected similar catastrophes over hundreds of years. Your bum may be out of your pants but it would be resting on real leather. Then there was the roulette wheel with two house numbers. Now, that was a real bummer.

Lady Luck smiled on me on that fateful afternoon in Monaco. I will not be so crude as to discuss the amount of my windfall but I could now afford a cup of coffee at the Four Seasons. I continued my journey with an Australian friend in tow. Well, she said she was Australian, although she had never set foot on our golden shores and didn't speak a word of English. Some people will say anything to get a ride to the border. I was half way through trying to explain about the luckiest day of my life when this mad Italian in a super-charged mini hit me amidships, at speed. His car bounced more than mine but he recovered faster. As did she. In no time at all, my faithful companion had transferred her indentures to the mini and they were both over the border before I had picked up all the pieces.

Some of you may get the impression that I am not a lucky person. When people talk about luck, they tend to sometimes forget the downside. There's good luck and there's bad luck. What I had that day was probably good fortune, followed by misfortune. What I had that evening was nothing. The bird had flown and I was stuck in a Menton pension with a bunch of geriatrics. I couldn't even see the television. There was a giant tree growing through the roof in the living room.

SAND IN MY SHOES

I have always wanted to travel to Egypt. At every opportunity I read all about the place. The other day I discovered this fantastic book in the library about the discoveries and excavations that were so prevalent in the twenties. I couldn't wait to take my hot milk to bed and discover all there is to know about the pyramids and their secrets. Unfortunately, it had been a tough day and I wasn't as resilient as I thought. I nodded off before I reached page five and woke up in this bloody big crater, surrounded by a group of smelly goat herders who were speaking in tongues. It was nice that they were trying to be friendly but their personal hygiene left a lot to be desired; they must have showered in camel piss.

Somehow, I had got myself into a bit of a hole and they were kind enough to get me out and direct me to the Sheikh Sunny Salem Guest House, which is run by a family of nomadic Bedouins for rich infidels like me. The fact that they were nomadic was a cause for concern. The management was never there when you needed them but always appeared from nowhere when you were ready to pay your bill.

The thing about the Pyramids is that they were just as big in the twenties as they are today. You were always tripping over archaeologists at some dig or other but I have to be perfectly honest. None of them looked remotely like Angelina Jolie, who is very much a Hollywood version of a contemporary crypt crawler. The first tomb raider that I met was a Brit called Howard Carter. We were at a small bar in Luxor and he said he was looking for some cache. I was a bit short, myself but I lent him ten quid and wished him good fortune. Two days later, he discovered Tutankhamen's Tomb.

Since we had become such good friends, Howard invited me over to see what he had uncovered but I had to pass. A mysterious intermediary had offered me the sweetest date that I could ever imagine for a small fee that on any other day would probably feed one hundred villages. The dark eyes behind the thin veil promised delights that I could only conjure up in my wildest dreams. It turned out to be the most expensive bowl of fruit that I have ever eaten. Still, that's the Arabs for you, isn't it? Nothing is what it seems and that's the way they like it. I can remember when I first saw that cinema classic: *The*

Desert Song. I never understood why the heroine couldn't work out that her male companion and the Riff leader were one and the same. They looked identical.

As a Jesuit-educated conservative, I am more beholden to Aloysius than Allah but these guys put on a good show and there is no doubt about their sincerity. There does, however, need to be a little work done on their chanting and the aforementioned Hollywood heart throb could well be commandeered to instill some variation to their vibrato. Did I tell you that they don't need alarm-clocks in Cairo? Before the sun comes up over the minarets, all eyes turn to Mecca and they seriously ramp up the volume on their incantations. My eyes are usually buried in a pillow with my ears, praying that a Celine Dion ballad comes up next.

I was not destined to see the golden treasures of the Pharaohs on this trip due to the untimely interruption of my own alarm clock, which brought me back to reality with a thud. I fell out of bed. You probably think that this isn't much of a bedtime story but I would be deluding you if I didn't confess to the fact that I have indeed marveled at these riches. They have been paraded around the world on a few occasions and I was fortunate enough to join the never-ending queue when Tutankhamen's trinkets made a whistle-stop in New Orleans in 1978. This was my first visit to the Deep South and I could only marvel at this most unique American city — so different to the rest of the country.

A city of irrepressible optimism!

In 2005, a gigantic hurricane just about wiped out *The Big Easy* but I am pleased to report that the natives have put the place back together again and everyone is pleased about that. New Orleans is a city with Desire, which is a funny name for a streetcar but Tennessee Williams just loved this town. His most seminal work first appeared on Broadway in 1947. In 1948, the tram route closed down. I'm not sure how he felt about that.

It is described as being wantonly seductive, oozing sensuality, decadence and depravity and not necessarily in that order. The burghers are even proud to declare it the most dangerous city in America. I love the word "oozes," so I couldn't wait to get there, in particular to that part of the city that is universally recognized as the home of jazz. Preservation Hall is rather basic. You put your money in the hat, close your eyes and listen to the music. The hallowed hall will then resonate to memories of Louis Armstrong and other immortals. The afore-mentioned trumpet and cornet player spread his magic through many generations and even the harmony handicapped youngsters of today will concede his legendary contribution to the music spectrum. What a wonderful world.

Armstrong was born and raised in New Orleans and his early musical career was consummated amidst the confusion of gangsters with machine guns, river boat dandies, bootlegging, speakeasies and fast money. It was the twenties and this was the best place to consume copious quantities of hard liquor and good tucker such as Jambalaya, Crawfish Pie and black-eyed peas. They even wrote songs about their food and the musicians were always suffering for their craft. Jelly Roll Morton and Fats Waller always licked their chops before their set.

Traditional Gumbo is a menu masterpiece and after you dribble some garlic butter sauce down your chin, you may get the urge to investigate the Creole or Cajun lifestyle. This will require a side trip to somewhere like Lafayette, which is a few hours from New Orleans, as the Ford Thunderbird flies. The Cajuns were displaced French Canadians who settled in the area in the seventeenth century. They brought with them their own brand of music and some great recipes. The Creoles were more French African and you can visit a typical Creole Plantation on a New Orleans bus tour. This particular part of Louisiana is called Acadiana and is a bit boggy. The locals mostly wear braces and are a very friendly lot. Unfortunately, the Moonshine in the Mountains Tour was discontinued after the film release of Deliverance but the Cajun Bayou Tour is still available and not to be missed.

New Orleans is a tourist magnet but if you've got it, why not flaunt it? Milk their history, absorb their culture and embrace their Ol' Man River. I don't know how many pees there are in Mississippi but if they keep serving those bourbon drinks in such large glasses… The Mardi Gras in January is also a great reason to visit this historic town. Stay in the French Quarter and you may be lucky to get to a masked ball or attend any number of parades over this period. If nudity offends, you may be embarrassed after the Grand Parade gets going on the final day, when the population of the city doubles. Some of those couturiers never seem to have enough material to complete their costumes.

People often tell me that I remind them a lot of Clark Gable and I know that he had quite a romantic attachment to the Deep South. In those quiet moments of reverie, I often imagine that I am promenading some ravishing southern belle past those old homes in the garden district. Naturally, she would be wearing a bonnet, carrying a parasol and bear a remarkable likeness to Vivien Leigh or Elizabeth Taylor. In reality, I ended up on a riverboat with a pair of queens. Sadly, the other guy had a straight flush and all I could do was drown my sorrows. Then she appeared out of nowhere. Very pretty. Very confident. I asked for her name. She said it was Eileen. *I lean on the bar and you buy the drinks.* Now, how romantic is that?

The war veteran!

The world-wise traveler knows that only when you arrive at your destination does the real bonus of your trip become obvious. It is all about meeting new people, whether they are fellow tourists, locals or charlatans on the make. I have met plenty of the latter but the most intriguing encounter of my southern excursion was with an ageless raconteur who was permanently propped up on the corner stool of a Bourbon St bar. To this day, I don't know what he was drinking but he always left with a pint to go. I believe that it may have been fuel for his motorcycle.

Clay Beauregard 111 was the unluckiest man that I have ever known. His friends called him Skip — probably because he always had to leave town in a hurry. In 1941, Skip had completed his first year of full employment which entitled him to two weeks paid leave. After much consultation, he decided that beach and sun was the way to go. Five minutes after landing at his destination, he concluded that this had been an inspired choice. He couldn't believe what a wonderful, pristine environment he was looking at. No wonder they called it Pearl Harbor.

Skip found his lodgings, checked in, signed up for a few tours and then decided to go for a walk. He didn't get far. All of a sudden, the chirping birds and blue skies above the Pacific Ocean disintegrated into a cacophony of airplane engines, guns, bombs and mayhem. He ran back to his hotel but it was no longer there. His appointment at the Japanese Bath House was also looking a bit shaky.

Being a patriot, the lad immediately signed up for active duty but asked to be dispatched to a different theater of war. He was no longer keen on beach and sun. This was a stance that he maintained until many years later a friend recommended a delightful spot called Muratoa Atoll. In retrospect, perhaps he wasn't a friend and there was a bit of professional jealousy there. He said it was French, very exclusive and out of the way, a bit. It was exclusive, all right. When they detonated their atomic bomb on the bloody place, Skip was the only inhabitant. Fortunately, he had been warned and was togged-up appropriately; in a boiler suit designed by Coco Chanel. Yes, you guessed it. There was no zipper.

I think that you get the general idea about Mr Beauregard and his bad luck. I have to say that these stories do seem a little less believable when reviewing them in the afterglow of sobriety. Perhaps I was just his perfect foil and ripe for persuasion. After all, the inevitability of disaster is part and parcel of the pessimist's code of life and I wear that mantle with conviction. Without prejudice, you would have to say that he was quite a character and I would certainly classify him as a unique personality.

It may be that you think that my entertainment options are limited if I need to seek the company of strangers in darkened bars and hospitality hell holes like the Dog and Wife Bar in Phuket, which I have yet to mention. You may be right but the truth of the matter is that these establishments are spokes in the wheel of life. When I sat down with Clay in New Orleans, it was a generation baton change. His race was almost run and yet there were so many untold stories. It reminds me of the advertising for that ground-breaking TV series *The Naked City*. The promo went something like this: *There are eight million stories in the Naked City and this is one of them.* One smart ass wrote in: *If there are so many stories, why are there so many bloody repeats?*

Did someone mention Thailand?

To the casual observer, aid programs in Thailand appear to demand little in the way of urgency, except for those contractual agreements that are indelibly linked to profitability. However, my friend had bedded down his project on time and found himself firmly entrenched on the ubiquitous bar stool at the Dog and Wife Bar on Patong Beach, Phuket. His boss, in a spirit of gratitude, had promised to spring for ten Pineapple Bombs, to be consumed in one sitting, air-fares included.

It was an implied agreement, stated and now to be consummated. Ten Pineapple Bombs is a tall order and I was there to help out.

Because posterity demands that moments in time are recorded for later reflection, I can tell you that it was the night of the Queen's Birthday. The lady in question was in her mid-sixties and revered by all. The management of the Dog and Wife Bar had concluded that as she was a mature and experienced woman with an understanding nature, she would readily forgive those who chose to ignore the alcohol ban that had been imposed by the local authorities for this day of days. However, they were out of pineapples.

In such a place, this was a minor problem, soon rectified. It wasn't long before the team behind the bar started doing what they did best. Making a Pineapple Bomb was no easy task and could hardly be left to one person. It involved coring, cutting, mixing, shaking, flower arranging and straw-bending. It gave them all something to do because apart from the omnipresent doll-faced whores, who were in reconnaissance mode, we were the only customers. The beauty of the Pineapple Bomb was that the whores wouldn't sit on your drink. They sat on everything else.

At some time, there may well have been an official recipe: a glutinous mix that would best blend with the aromatic juices of the fruit to provide the ultimate in mellifluous ecstasy. At the Dog and Wife, they had arrived at a high-octane potion that surely had multiple uses. In fact, I was wondering if Skip Beauregard had been here with his Yamaha. Nevertheless, the Bombs were always served with the required amount of ritualistic ceremony because there was little doubt that we were movers and shakers of the highest order. I don't remember much after that but, as I saw it, we never did achieve the ten bombs required to be consumed in one sitting. As a bonding session, one could not complain and, in all modesty, I think we became corporate trailblazers. Today, company executives don't just go to the board room for a meeting. No siree, Bob! They take fifteen people with spouses to the Caribbean, put them up in deluxe accommodation and then fly them home first class. The shareholders don't seem to mind a bit.

The bottom line!

Contemporary progressive countries like America, Sweden and Germany no longer rate dinosaurs like me and my fellow trailblazers. They have information technology. Their key people will take a lap-top to bed rather than a good book or an insatiable nymphomaniac. Where is the romance? From the shifting sands of the Sahara to the murky mudflats of the Mississippi, exploration and opportunity awaits you; but first, you've got to get out of the house.

If you can't get on one of those corporate junkets, why not try a bit of adventure tourism? There are still mountains to be scaled, rivers to be crossed and any number of bridges to jump off. The organizers are only too happy to push you out of airplanes and submerge you in shark infested waters. If you see your bank manager on the other side of the cage, a weak smile will be more than appropriate.

You may meet me by chance somewhere along the way. I will probably be heading in the opposite direction but perhaps we can share a jar if you survive whatever experience you have signed on for. A man with memories can sometimes make the minutes feel like hours and that's the kind of guy that I am. Let me tell you how I ran with the bulls in Pamplona and if this excites you, please ask to see one of my tattoos, which commemorates the occasion.

My final advice is that you'll need to do it before it is too late. Otherwise, you may end up being careful and sensible and wearing comfortable undies. We can't have that, can we?

– 6 –

PEOPLE I HAVE KNOWN

The two of us

The old man and the bee

Food for thought

My friend, the serial killer

Some of you may be a little dubious about my relationships with the folks who occupy the following pages. Just because you know somebody doesn't mean that you are friends with them.

Nevertheless, you are drawn to people. I have known certain individuals whose lifestyle and standard of morality are abhorrent to me. Yet, I crave the opportunity to be part of their intimate coterie. If you have never been a social climber, you will never understand this.

There is nothing special about the good citizens that you are going to read about. They just got caught up in my crosshairs and their lives are no longer a secret. More's the pity.

THE TWO OF US

Basil and Rosemary were meant for each other. At least, that's the way the salivating stud from Sandringham saw it. Bazza was precariously perched on the penultimate pew at St Andrews Bar and Grill. In a previous life, the establishment had been a holy temple. Now it was a Kirk with a kick, offering solace to saints, sinners and sycophantic toads with a thirst for camaraderie and companionship. In short, it was a pick-up joint.

You could never mistake Basil for a saint. After all, he was an advertising man; the very trendy gear and sleazy grin gave him away. Rosemary picked it in one but there was little time for further analysis because he was heading in her direction and coming on strong. The young woman recoiled from the alcoholic zephyr that was his breath. Had he bathed in bourbon?

The thing was that she was hot and he was a combustible ethane, looking for a flame. The gossamer of sheer silk that loosely covered her slender waist was brushed aside as his confident fingers embarked on a voyage of discovery towards the inner recesses of her aerobically maintained thighs. She had met fast movers before but he hadn't even introduced himself and all this under the patronizing gaze of the hapless St Andrew. The statue had been too big to move so they left it there.

If she wanted a diversion, there was none coming. The rowdy group of accountants who had been bonding earlier in the evening had long disappeared. Even the barman was missing. Was Rosemary imagining things or had somebody hit the dimmer switch? From a solitary speaker above her head, the muted sound of a Miles Davis trumpet solo cut into the foreboding silence like a fart at a chamber music recital. Rosie was teetering on the last bar stool and there was no retreat. Literally, she had her back to the wall.

If you thought that Rosemary was incapable of handling the likes of Basil and his macho come-on, you would be wrong. Let's face it. She was in the rock-ape business herself and hadn't she that very day stitched up a lucrative house and land package with two perplexed pensioners from Prahran? Now, they were just a mere ninety minutes from the nearest medical facility and bingo hall.

Rosie was some kind of lady. Her penetrating blue eyes were like two incandescent pools of liquid innocence, which was completely lost on Basil. He had his own baby blues firmly transfixed on her gently heaving breasts, only a heartbeat and a home run away from her bent straw. His own straw was no longer bent. He was in love but not unappreciative of the task ahead. This chick was formidable: intelligent, articulate, and an athlete, gourmet cook and an opinionated art critic. She could also be very intimidating: *Basil Baby, where did you get that poncy pink shirt? It sucks.*

It may seem incredulous but Basil actually got to first base although a long way off a home run. Somehow there was a bit of a spark generated but if Rosemary had received the wrong type of invitation, there would definitely be no ignition. Fortunately, the man did the right thing and invited her to dinner. Basil was on good terms with the management of a pleasant little bistro in a swank part of town and Rosie was a pushover for all things gastronomic.

It takes a while to get to know someone and she really didn't know whether he was cheap or just clever. The man insisted that because she was in real estate they should order a house wine. If she was really hungry, you couldn't beat the Hungarian Goulash. This was also the least expensive dish on the menu. The fact is that Basil took the view that expenditure should be reliant on reward and at this stage of the evening, he wasn't sure that they were going to make out, as they say in the classics.

On the other side of the table, Rosemary was a person who never tired of listening to someone who is well-read, widely traveled, interesting, witty and creatively accomplished. Tonight, she had to listen to Basil, who had lurched into a dissertation on the great writers of our time. Unfortunately, Scott Fitzgerald, John Steinbeck and Jack Kerouac didn't get a look in. They were all advertising people, with the exception of Kinky Friedman, Joan Collins and Naomi Campbell. After their third bottle of wine, Basil was well into his bullshit the bimbo routine: *This red is decidedly full-bodied, Rosemary. What a delicate nose! It reminds me so much of you.*

Most girls would rather die than date a dag in a poncy pink shirt but history does tell us that opposites attract and in fact, they sometimes make strange bedfellows. So it was with Basil and Rosemary. Although the Chocolate Refrigerator Cake looked sensational, they didn't wait around for dessert. The maître d' and the chef bid farewell to the young couple with a smug and knowing look on their faces. Yet another victory for good food and an over indulgence in alcohol.

They say that the night has a thousand eyes and the next morning Rosie felt a large pang of pain behind two of them. The other nine hundred and ninety eight were lowered in a gesture of remorse and recrimination. What has not been previously revealed is that the lady had a boyfriend; the quick tempered Justin.

Unfortunately, Justin couldn't make it to St Andrews Bar and Grill because he had to visit his sick mother upcountry. What was even more unfortunate was the fact that Carol, her flat mate, had seen her go off with Basil and would be aware that bed-making chores would not be required in their apartment that morning. Carol also had a mouth like a parrot on Pentothal.

Up until now, Justin has been a background figure in this whole saga. You've heard about his violent temper but you know little else. You haven't sat in his black Porsche, sipping a glass of chilled Krug as Rosemary had, or stroked his tight buns as he slipped down from Nefertiti, the only Albino Polo Pony on the eastern seaboard. You never will. Justin chose to leave this heart stopping melodrama in a fit of pique. He arrived on schedule for their date that night but Rosie's outstretched hand, expecting the chrome and polished paintwork of Germany's finest, found nothing but air. With a screech of burning rubber and an orgasmic thrust of throbbing horsepower, Rosemary was left in a state of suspended animation. Justin had done a bunk. She would never see him again.

In the weeks that followed Justin's departure, Basil and Rosemary only had eyes for each other. They did the town in style: frolicking in the French Quarter and slumming it at Greasy Joes. They dined on the Restaurant Tram and threw down Martinis and Mai Tais. She chose his ties and he washed her car. It was enough to make Basil's friends sick and disgusted. Another poor bastard caught in the old Beaver Trap. On 18 February, exactly six weeks and two days since their first meeting, Rosemary moved into Albuquerque Avenue.

It was a foggy day in Melbourne town, the day that Rosemary moved into apartment seven at sixty-nine Albuquerque Avenue. The letterbox signage had already been amended to accommodate the new tenant. It read: *Mr Basil Bartholomew and Ms Rosemary Cahill: New Age Couple.*

Rosie was neatly balanced on the edge of her last packing case, contemplating the move. Would this be the end of her personal freedom as she knew it? Had she done the right thing? Should she have waited a little longer? Her brother was helping with the transport. Lance didn't get out much and watched too much television — mainly talent quests and game shows. However, he did own a pick-up truck and that was convenient. *Well, Basil! There it is. All my belongings. I'm now in residence.*

Gee, sweetheart! There's so much. I thought you traveled light. Hey, Lance! Watch that table. It's expensive. Of course, that table was first on Rosie's dump list along with Basil's favorite chair, his monkey-pod carvings and framed Gorilla-Gram. His collection of international beer cans was also doomed and earmarked for the scrapheap. *There is a lot, isn't there? A bit of duplication, too. Don't worry, pet. I'll make a list and we'll have a garage sale.* The thing about lists is that the only one that survives is the one prepared by a female hand. Most of the lad's prize possessions found their way to surprised and amused recipients — all purchased for a small percentage of their true value. One man's trash is another man's treasure.

Basil didn't like Lance a lot and was relieved when he excused himself and returned to his lonely existence in the hinterland. *Thank God that drone has gone. Really, Rosie! I can't believe he's your brother. Was there mental illness in the family?*

If you thought that the first few hours of Basil and Rosemary's co-habitation was a little testy, you'd be absolutely right. But then again, these were testing times. There was groundwork to be laid, parameters to be established and egos to be cut down to size. Were they the perfect couple? Who knows? They were certainly in the same orchestra but we all know who was playing second fiddle.

Rosie really is something else. I'll never be able to bring the boss home for dinner. She's already here. Assertive, strong-willed and very confident! Do you know she even does her crosswords in ink? Can you believe that? Still, I think this living together thing will work out. I know that we took that compatibility test and I failed but that's Rosie for you. Not everyone objects to a home-brew kit in the bathroom.

For Basil and Rosemary, the first day of the rest of their life finished with a whimper rather than a bang, although it certainly had its moments. The undisguised animosity between Basil and Lance did not auger well for the future, especially as Rosie's brother would be a house guest on many future occasions. After all, he did live out of town and he was a blood relative. Couldn't Basil understand that? Basil could understand what he wanted to understand. This was a position that he took and it worked effectively to diminish Rosie's favored status as a confident know-all.

You know, a lot of people think that Rosie is the dominant partner in our relationship and I can appreciate their feelings. They say that she wants you to have opinions of your own but doesn't want to hear them. These kinds of comments are thoughtless and unkind. Rosie is a very caring individual — admittedly, with delusions of grandeur. I can live with that. After all, every day she has to prove herself in a man's world and sharing her victories with me sometimes doesn't stimulate the adulation she is looking for.

Basil, did I tell you that I topped the sales figures again this month? McCurry and Sandy Rice were livid. They just can't cope with being beaten by a woman.

That's nice, dear. Tell me, have you seen the TV guide?

Let's hear it for the good old mind-games. Basil played them well and when Rosie's frustrations became obvious, there was always that smug smile that indicated a moral victory. Nevertheless, such is not the basis for love and commitment that is steadfast and uncompromising.

It had been a number of weeks since Basil and Rosemary set up their love nest and things had been pretty rocky on the home trail. Then again, wasn't this what we expected? Basil was the problem. Although he was the chief instigator of this cozy co-habitation, he hadn't anticipated the sacrifices that would have to be made. Helplessly, he watched as all his favorite possessions were junked, compacted or re-cycled. His wardrobe was still trendy but uncomfortable and all his mates high-tailed it whenever they saw Rosie coming.

Was she so intimidating? Or had he just dropped his bundle? For so long, he was the master of his own destiny. A more confident man you would never hope to know. A few months earlier, if you had seen Basil sitting in a crowded bus, he'd probably be flirting with a woman who was standing. Now, his insecurities were starting to show. He knew it was time to get back on top. The dinner party with Tom and Geraldine would be the perfect opportunity.

There is always something cathartic about a dinner party. Usually, someone feels the urge to purge their soul, denigrate their closest friends and make a complete and utter ass of themselves. Usually, it would be Basil. This night it would be Geraldine who scaled the heights of impropriety, embraced the god of vitriol and let go with an assortment of invectives that had Tom gagging on his guacamole dip. They were both friends of Rosemary which made the episode even sweeter.

Gerry, would you like some white wine with your duck? Or will you stay with the B47 cocktail **that Basil mixed for you**?

Thank you, Rosie. I like wine with duck. In fact, I like it without duck, too.

Approximately twenty minutes before Geraldine threw-up, Basil knew that he was for the high jump. Rosie was ropeable. Who else would have the nerve to give the lush with the long legs a stiff bourbon with a vodka teaser and a maraschino cherry dipped in Drambui? Basil claims that he didn't know she drank until he saw her sober.

Tom and Gerry

For now, he was chewing the fat with Tom, pretending to be impervious to Rosemary's accusatory glance in his direction. Nevertheless, this silent denunciation was as uncompromising as a guillotine hurtling down on its journey of destruction. This was Rosie with her Irish up and didn't he love it? Sure, she wants him to feel like a contrite axe-murderer but I have to tell you, the madder she gets, the more randy he gets.

My God, when are these people going home?

The complexities of the Basil and Rosemary relationship were never more apparent than the night of the infamous Tom and Geraldine dinner party. Basil had arrived home from the office determined to shore up his waning confidence and found himself unwittingly thrown into someone else's nightmare. Whilst Geraldine lost the plot and Rosemary lost her cool, Basil somehow acquired an inner strength from their display of female fragility. Who could understand why? True, a man who spends his working life trying to sell ice to Eskimos is sure to take advantage of a crack in the iceberg. Or was it because he was simply a chauvinistic pig?

Basil would be less than honest if he didn't admit to enjoying Gerry's performance. She made a complete and utter ass of herself. Obviously, Tom had seen it all before. However, Rosie was in a real stew. After all, she usually relied on Gerry to be complimentary about the magnificent meal, to discuss the stuffing ingredients and to review the aftertaste. Obviously an ego thing but an essential part of Rosemary's complex mentality. It was, therefore, an unmitigated disaster that Gerry, in her advanced state of inebriation, couldn't tell whether she was eating duck or muck. Bazza would have to hand in his cocktail mixer's license and apologize to Rosie. It wouldn't be easy but the recriminations never lasted long and the make-up sex was great.

There is no reason to continue this tale any further. You all know how it will end. The encounter of Basil and Rosemary was a typical tryst that is as predictable as it was tedious. The passion that precedes every romantic relationship is the high point that can never be repeated. Basil and Rosemary will end up like Tom and Gerry. Lance may have had a chance with Susan Boyle but now she is a superstar. It is all so depressing.

Everybody is trying to take the spice out of life. Recently, they found a relic in the back bar of St Andrews and it wasn't Bill Cosby. They had to cancel the liquor license and once again establish Christian procedures. The re-consecrated church is now run by an order of devout nuns but I like to think that it might still be a fun place to visit. The cute young novitiates are the best people to see. Ask for Ginger or Saffron.

THE OLD MAN AND THE BEE

When my old friends and acquaintances pass on, I always like to take time to reflect on their achievements. The farewell service will always unearth some previously unknown fact that will shock or surprise. So it was with Arthur, an old friend in the truest sense of the word. He was one of the few non-Americans who called his wife Honey. That's because it was her name: Honey Ryder. Ring any bells?

Sure, he called her Queen Bee and why not? Their union was his third trip to the altar and her fourth, so they were mature individuals who knew what was ahead of them. Arthur had actually known Honey for years. He was attached to the Foreign Office in the Bahamas during the fifties when she got involved in that fracas with that arrogant secret agent James Bond and his nemesis, the despicable Dr No. I seem to recall that she was a bit of a collector — sea shells, I think.

They were married in the Putney Registry Office and from that day forward, he was the one who had to shell out — makeovers, facelifts, tummy tucks, a boob job and the usual visits to the clinic for Botox and detox. He discovered that a late marriage is a whole new ball game. Nevertheless, she wanted for nothing and he was pleased to oblige. Rich people can be so accommodating.

There is some conjecture as to how Arthur got rich. I can remember when he was my case officer at MI6. He operated from modest digs in the West End of London and used to take his holidays in Benidorm. In fact, he met his first wife there. She was some sort of Spanish countess and we were a bit surprised as she wasn't a great beauty. He kind of disappeared after that and started dabbling in black ops stuff — undetectable poisons, I believe. By co-incidence, his new bride died rather suddenly and this must have shocked him.

When the man re-emerged from obscurity, he had become the social darling of the Embassy set and was always seen with a stunning blonde on his arm. Strangely, his next wife was rather plain: the only child of a highly successful condom manufacturer from Delhi. She was to last no longer than her predecessor but slightly longer than her father. When I heard that the cause of death was food poisoning, I begged off curries for life.

Meanwhile, back at the beehive!

Although more transparent, Honey's life journey was also complicated. Her romance with Bond was short-lived and the reason that it had no legs was the fact that he usually had his legs entwined elsewhere. *All in the line of duty* he said but I expect that even Queen and country were skeptical. The lady hooked up with a marine biologist called George Costanza and she seemed to be on the path to contentment and happiness. Alas, it turned out to be a rocky road. The nuptials were held in New York, where she met some of his seriously deranged friends and, in the light of day, realized that she had made a big mistake. It wasn't that George was a bad bagel or anything like that but the whole situation was weird. His parents were actually certifiable.

Honey hit the highway and re-surfaced in Paris. She had always been a bit arty and life on the Left Bank in the City of Light suited her. Naturally, she socialized with the avant-garde and frequented all the salons and havens of artistic merit. She found piece work and actually forged out a living by designing bikinis for Pierre Cardin. In those days, Paris was a reasonable place to live. You could buy simple things without having to mortgage your house. Bon Marché. Only the affluent could be extravagant and they were frequently indulgent. They would pay obscene prices for highly inedible substances that were sold in small cans or large jars. In some cases, the contents were still growing and the more horrible the smell, the more expensive the product.

Honey had simple tastes and etched out quite a comfortable existence in her small apartment in the shadows of Napoleon's Tomb. She often remarked: *He was such a small fellow. Why did they build him such a big tomb?* I think that she liked this city, rather than loved it. Of course, her real love was sea shells and Paris really wasn't much of a place for that. She eventually moved to Marseille but only indirectly. In later years, Arthur would tell many stories about how he always ragged his wife about her religious beliefs. Her favorite saint was St Emilion and it was on her way to Marseille that she first encountered divine intervention: amongst the Merlot producing vines of Bordeaux.

It is not down to me to comment on her drinking habits but it is fair to say that she did like a tipple. It took her seven months to cover the modest journey to the port city and she only moved on due to total embarrassment. Someone had released a song entitled *Lady in Red* and one of the local pranksters had rewritten the words, which pointed accusingly at her. Quite frankly, I couldn't understand the fuss. A lot of people have wine for breakfast. I am not one who would approve of besmirching one's reputation because I realize that we all have skeletons in the closet. If you opened my wardrobe, you would find a whole graveyard inside.

Honey made a real go of it in what was a pretty rough city. It wasn't long before she attracted suntanned suitors from the suburban settlements around snob hill. The end story was predictable and dare I say it, inevitable.

Honey's second husband was an articulate aristocrat with vested interests far and wide. She moved into his palatial mansion in the hills around Grasse, convenient to both Marseille and the Riviera. This is the area where French perfume originates and it is a veritable panorama of perfection. Arthur and I were regulars at the Cannes Film Festival and we used to run into her quite often. She would gush forth in her delightful Scandinavian accent: *Darlings, we must do lunch*. It mattered not that we were already at lunch and she was onto her fifth glass of champagne. Of course, this was all before her husband was unmasked as the Mr Big of the largest drug cartel in the country. He had locked horns with a foul-mouthed New York cop called Popeye Doyle and came off second best. They put him in the slammer and that is where he stayed for the rest of his days.

You have to be resilient to bounce back from something like this. Naturally, they confiscated all his earthly possessions and that meant that Honey Ryder was looking for another meal ticket. And she was not getting any younger. Now, you are probably going to jump in and say: *Arthur is still there at the film festival. Go get him girl*. Of course, you have gone off half-cocked and one husband too early.

Honey with no breadwinner!

G'day mate.

I have known quite a few bookmakers and their generosity of spirit is without question. They are less generous when considering the possible and offsetting it against the probable. Still, you could have acquired very long odds about our favorite shell collector marrying an Australian. I don't even know how she got to our fair country. The last two Europeans who tried to visit me ended up in Melbourne, Florida. I have no doubt that when she did get here, she would have been captivated — endless white sand, coral reefs, hunky lifesavers and there were irresistible swells everywhere. The surf was good too but unfortunately, she didn't quite fill out a bikini as in days gone by. Too many of those French pastries, I suppose.

It wasn't long before she whipped herself into shape and got herself a job aboard one of those charter vessels in the Whitsundays.

A bareboat charter is where they rent you their yacht or catamaran and hope that you can sail it. The alternative is a crewed craft with a Captain and Hostess supplied. She cooks, does drinks and smiles a lot — very similar to the first two months of the average marriage.

When she heard that I was back in the country, I was invited up north. Now, I'm not a sailor. Never have been. As a young lad, I read the works of Jules Verne and Herman Melville but I preferred W.E. Johns. My most indelible memory is that of Biggles, Algy and Ginger ditching in the Ionian Sea after a nasty confrontation with a German Messerschmitt. My childhood heroes always made it but I'm not a lucky person. Who was it that compared a sailing boat to a jail where you can drown?

But The Whitsundays are something else — over seventy magic islands, dipped in an azure sea and garnished with tropical vegetation, sun-dried beaches and colorful coral reef fish. For a frozen Victorian, nine hundred kilometers north of Brisbane seemed like a nice place to be. So I accepted her invitation and we had a great time. She took me out in the boat and I can tell you, folks: *Do it and you will not regret the experience.* When it's all over, you'll have fond memories of a great holiday and names like Hook Island, Butterfly Bay and Humpy Point will be entrenched in your memory long after your fifth pregnancy, accelerated interest rates and your forthcoming bankruptcy.

We dined, of course, and partied continuously. I stayed longer than I should have but what the heck. On the seventh day we got married. Another big mistake! I had never been married before and didn't realize all the things that are unacceptable post-ceremony. She claimed that I snored too much, farted too much and never replaced the lid on the loo. Surely, these are the traditional rights of all Australian males. We were divorced three days later and I quickly dispatched an email to the Pope, to try and determine whether he was prepared to forget the whole thing.

I think that MI6 must have been bugging the Vatican because in no time at all, Arthur was on the phone, wanting to know what had happened. I was calling her a B this and a B that and a drama queen to boot. That's when Arthur decided that we should call her the Queen Bee. He convinced me to mend the bridges and I'm glad that I did. We made up but parted ways. She had to leave anyway. The company's most important client nearly choked on one of her sushi entrees and then she accidently pushed him overboard and he drowned. I suggested that she repatriate herself to the old country, which she did — right into Arthur's arms.

Arthur was a man of many parts and some would say that he was a little two-faced. But he was not an absolute cad. With Honey, he slipped into tea and sympathy mode but left the bedroom door ajar should the divorcée require extra sympathy. Being a long-standing covert operative, he was conversant with all manner of interrogation, rendition and the most insidious subterfuge of them all — the Honey Pot. This form of entrapment requires one to use sexual favors as an inducement to compromise a target and Arthur was good at it. Not that Honey had many secrets other than her age. It wasn't long before he had stripped her bare: her mind, her body and her meager superannuation funds from the Sea Shell Preservation Society. Not that he needed the money. He just couldn't help himself.

They were eventually married and enjoyed fifteen good years together. Arthur Wilson retired from the service with a virtual knighthood (you're not allowed to tell anybody) and moved to the country, where he proceeded to go downhill fast. He became rather obnoxious in his old age. He was always grumpy and would find fault in everything his wife did. Towards the end, the boys down at the local were betting on the eventual manner of his demise. Not surprisingly, food poisoning was two to one favorite. As often as not, the bookies are always right.

To celebrate his seventy-fifth birthday, Honey thought that she would make him a special meal: her very own sushi delight. She decided that no expense would be spared on the ingredients and went shopping for the most expensive fish on the market. Now, I suppose you know where this is heading. The apprentice at the Japanese Supermarket sold Honey a deadly Blow Fish by mistake. It is the greatest delicacy and the most expensive but because of its lethal nature, only qualified chefs are allowed to prepare it. To cut a long story short, he sampled the seductive sushi and expired on the spot. Thank God, Honey didn't feel obliged to try it. I think that she was still on a guilt trip after her Australian experience.

With Arthur gone, Honey and I didn't see much of each other, although we did catch up occasionally. I made a point of doing the cooking. The last I heard of her, she had joined MI6 through the dead partners program. Obviously, Bond had retired because I couldn't see those two getting together again.

When you are deep-cover for any intelligence service, you have probably been anointed with what they term a legend. This is a false identity that has been scripted to survive the most severe scrutiny. It will detail your imaginary life in great detail and is supported by forged passports, social security documents, credit cards and birth certificates. This is what she does. She puts together bogus identities for their agents. I am proud of her. We were only married for three days but it looks like I've taught her everything I know.

FOOD FOR THOUGHT

There are not many people who can afford the delights of the Grand Hotel in Venice. If they could, they would certainly dine on the terrace at the water's edge and savor Chef Roberto's legendary Involtini di Vitello. This wonderful veal dish is a specialty of the house and a memorable experience for those who order it.

Rosemary Cahill had nodded off. She often did that in the afternoon and for good reason. She had been up early for a power breakfast and this was followed by a power sales meeting, a motivational gathering with her peers and lunch with a client. Many people in real estate don't take alcohol with their lunch but Rosie maintained that she could handle it if restricted to Monday, Wednesday and Friday. It was Friday.

Our busy girl had recently moved in with her boy-friend and although Basil had initially been a bit of an excitement machine, things had become rather dreary. So, over lunch, she gave the Valpolicella a bit of a nudge and although the pasta at the local trattoria wasn't a patch on the Grand Hotel, it was enough to stimulate fond memories of a Neapolitan nature. Basil would not have been pleased.

Ahhh, yes! Rosie's student days in Italy! She was completely mesmerized by the art scene and every moment was a memory. In Venice, who wouldn't be besotted by the romanticism of the whole place? She was young and ready to be loved and because she had perky little tits and tight buns, one could always expect more than a pinch of salt when she hit the bistros and bars that surround the magnificent piazza that is St Mark's Square.

Enter Prince Alfredo Donatello DeMarco. What a charmer! Rosie had heard bullshit before and that dubious tale about his international search for the perfect woman was rather lame. Five would get you ten that he had a fat mama at home and six bouncing bambinos. She also seriously doubted his credentials at the palace but still considered him a real prince because he took her to the Grand Hotel; and yes, they dined on Involtini di Vitello.

To cut a long story short, the extended lunch and the short nap had given her the incentive to surprise her man with one of her special dinners. She found Roberto's recipe in one of their many cookbooks and because of it, beautiful Basil, the love of her life, would dine in style that night.

Here comes Basil now, the last of the romantics. He'll swan in, all smiles. Maybe some flowers. He'll be tantalized by the kitchen smells, congratulate the chef, put his hands down my pants and give me one of his now famous wet kisses. What a guy.

What a prick of a day. Can you believe it? They were all jerks. And those Nazi storm troopers! They towed my car. Is there no justice? Did I stiff a Chinaman or something?

Hello, darling. What's that horrible smell?

Oh dear! It looks like the new business pitch didn't go well. Nevertheless, our hero isn't one to dwell on misfortune and it wasn't long before he noticed the candles, Chianti and the focaccia — all spread out like a Tuscan picnic.

I do believe it is Italian night. Hey, what have we here: Involtini di Vitello?

My God! You recognize the Involtini. You've had it before?

Sure thing, sugar lips. An agency trip to Venice, a few years ago. Some scruffy little bistro by the water. It was as cheap as chips but good all the same. Bloody good!

It had never occurred to Rosemary that Basil might also have done Venice. It didn't seem like his kind of place. Of course, he probably didn't have any choice. A job was a job and why not Italy? On reflection, perhaps he would get by. The moonlit gondola rides would be an irresistible temptation — especially, if he found the right woman. Rosie made a mental note to ask him about that. She was sure that he would have no interest in the architecture and art treasures of Rome and Naples and definitely no inclination to visit the Leaning Tower. However, maybe Italy did hold a special interest for her favorite man.

He would certainly devour their soups and pasta with undisguised zeal and their many magnificent wines would all be sampled: Lambrusco, Orvieto, Frascati; he would be in the grip of the grape and loving it.

Darling, what can I say? This is superb. The melted ricotta seeping through this delicate pan-fried rolled veal. Wow! How do you do it? This is better than Venice.

What about your dining companion, lover? Am I better than what's her name....Antonia?

You mean Angelica. Well, it's hard to comp — I don't remember telling you about Angelica.

Women just love it when they can hang you out to dry — not that Basil was starting to squirm or anything like that. After all, why should he feel guilty? He hadn't even met her then. All the same, Rosie hated to think that he was actually having fun before she came along. Go figure.

A lot of people wonder how Basil and Rosie ever connected. They had little in common. She is so suave, sophisticated and artistically bent. He's just bent. You know: the footy, a beer with the boys, a cultural vacuum etc. But he is terribly handsome, unbelievably confident and just dripping with sex-appeal. Friends questioned her sanity when she moved in with Basil. Did somebody say he was a megalomaniac with an inferiority complex? How deftly put. You do have to massage his ego every so often but Rosie is an honors graduate in the art of male manipulation. He really is out of his depth — lost in the aura of her domination.

About this time, Rosemary made the sale of her life: a multi-million dollar bay-side auction. It was the turning point in her professional career and her reputation was enhanced no end. Even some of the old stagers were disposed to a bit of professional envy. For Rosie, it gave her renewed confidence in her abilities and replenished her hunger and enthusiasm. Of course, the work-load increased and because of this, Basil often found that he was now the first one home, after a hard day at the office.

Although he saw himself as a sensitive new age guy and proudly espoused his support for affirmative action and other women-on-top agencies that were politically correct, he never considered that he would get caught in the kitchen for more than a few token spaghetti dinners. He was wrong.

It's me, Basil. Sorry I'm late. What's for dinner?

Well, blue eyes! The cupboard is a bit bare, so I thought we'd eat out tonight. Perhaps Eve's Grill and Grind? They do great spare ribs.

Very tempting, Basil but we've dined out the last three nights. And what do you mean: the cupboard's bare? I shopped yesterday and we have enough food to feed Rwanda for a year.

Yeah! But who wants to eat Indian? You know it gives me wind.

By now, some of you may have recognized some disturbing traits in our hero's work ethic and his lack of devotion in sharing the load may be consistent with similar mannerisms that you have observed in the man that you married. I am sure that you are also shocked at his inept appreciation of geography and his crude attempt to drag Rosie off to Eve's is totally inappropriate. After all, it is a strip joint.

The last time I looked, super-brain, Rwanda was in Africa.

The next time I look, I want to see you in the kitchen; I'm going to take a shower.

Wow! The Gestapo really missed out with that one. If she had been born a few years earlier, the war could have produced a completely different result.

Basil rummaged around in their big drawer of cook books and recipes and come up with something that he thought would be appropriate — *Cooking secrets of the Third Reich*. Frankfurt with sauerkraut and mash! He was convinced that this would put hairs on Rosie's chest. To make an occasion of the meal, he ducked down to his local liquor outlet for some imported German beer and ferreted out his two oversized steins which would give the meal some level of authenticity. Unfortunately, it was not enough. The Bratwurst dinner was a disaster. The bangers caught fire and they shrunk alarmingly. Not only was his sausage shriveled, the cabbage tasted sour and the new potatoes looked very old. Secretly, Basil was hoping that this display of male incompetence might ensure a permanent ban from the kitchen but hope springs eternal. Rosemary was adamant that he could tidy up his act. She wasn't convinced that he hadn't perpetrated the disaster on purpose.

So they went to Eve's after all and Basil was almost beside himself. Mike Tyson was there with bruised ribs. Perhaps it was braised ribs?

Two mugs and the Cup!

Rosie had traveled. She was well-read, articulate and a successful businesswoman but it wasn't always that way. Ten years earlier, she was stuck in a small country town and it was horrible. If you didn't get married, you were an outcast and whenever the proposals were in the offing, she always came second. This kind of thing is never good for your self-esteem. She had worked on that and the result was there for all to see. Nevertheless, it would be soul-destroying if she couldn't get the guy and keep him. So, Basil was a very important work-in-progress.

Who would have believed it? Behind that superior exterior, here was somebody who knew that French fries were really chips. If Basil's friends had discovered that Rosie used to be Harriet Hayseed, there would be great mirth and humiliation. It was therefore necessary to keep up appearances and there was no more appropriate forum than the Spring Racing Carnival.

Basil, we're going to the Melbourne Cup.

It is hard to describe the madness that is the Melbourne Cup. A visitor from outer space would be totally mystified. For the locals, it is the day of days. A horse race that stops the nation. Basil and Rosemary would be in the Nursery Car Park, where a roast rabbit ragout from the rear of a roller is the only way to go. Overseas and interstate visitors abound in numbers. You can tickle the taste-buds with a tantalizing terrine off a trestle table and tear at some turkey with a terrible twit from Tipperary.

Gee, Rosie, if we are going to The Cup, why don't we do it properly? Let's take a chance and splurge on something. Big bucks; on the nose!

You mean... bet.

Of course I mean bet. You don't think the race is put on just for you to parade your fancy duds, do you?

Well, er!

Rosie changed her mind five times about the advisability of attending the big event. What if everything wasn't right? After all, she was now a bigwig in the real estate world and you have to seen to be in complete control. Of course, this was a total misrepresentation of the way that things really were. It was obvious that she had never attended Flemington before. In point of fact, everything seemed out of control.

Basil, how can we go? We don't have a proper picnic basket and René and Linda don't drink anything but French Champagne. And I don't have a thing to wear.

OK honey! That makes sense. Let's not go.

Not go! Basil, are you mad? This is the highlight of the social season. Everyone will be there. I'll be able to wear my new hat.

But, Rosie, love of my life, didn't you just tell me that you had nothing to wear?

Poor Basil! Is he from another planet or what? She hasn't brought her new hat yet — not to mention her gloves, a new summer dress, matching shoes, a Ferragamo scarf and a practical but eye-catching leather hand-bag.

You'll have to fork out, too, Basil. We'll need a new picnic basket, plastic crockery in designer colors, an assortment of vegan pâtés, other new-age deli items such as pink salmon, octopus, caviar and some bagels for our Jewish friends.

We don't have any Jewish friends.

Not now, darling but after I've spent megabucks on my new outfit, I expect to have a kibbutz named after me.

You wouldn't believe it but a horse called Kibbutz won one of the main races and true to his stated intentions, Basil bet up big on the animal. Champagne flowed freely all afternoon and the bagels soaked up the slops brilliantly.

Back at sixty-nine Albuquerque Avenue in the aftermath of the afternoon, things had been a bit testy. Basil was now in dreamland, passed out on a feather bed of hundred dollar notes. I suppose it was inevitable that he would get plastered (a horse of this name had won the Derby twelve months earlier) but it was the manner of his inebriation that had riled Rosemary. For some reason Basil always became very musical when he drank too much. In the early part of the day, the lady was fairly compliant as he crooned in her ear: *You're the cream in my coffee.* However, as the shadows were getting longer, the successful punter scrambled onto the bonnet of René's roller and belted out a half decent version of a Fats Waller favorite: *You're not the only oyster in the stew.* Rosie was rather rattled.

Bazza was also establishing a very chummy kind of liaison with the attractive jockey of the moment and had actually invited her home. Being completely sober and the designated driver, Mrs Fuehrer thanked the lass for her inspired ride and dropped her off at the nearest railway station. Under advisement, Basil slipped her an Igloo ($100) and of his own volition, gave her a further reward: a left over bagel for Kibbutz. So much for the spring races. Rosie wondered whether it was worth all the trouble. Basil had other ideas. Didn't he always?

Gee hun, that was great. Why don't we go to the Kentucky Derby next year? I believe those Mint Juleps are fantastic.

Indeed, they did do Kentucky and from there traveled to New York, the birth place of Fats Waller, where the food was superb and the music was inspirational. Theirs was a lifestyle that was much admired but they needed to do these things before thoughts turned to family matters. It was only a matter of time before young Herb would come along. After all, Rosemary's clock was ticking.

I read somewhere that some klutz thought that they were boring and predictable. What a moron. Half the young people on this planet would kill to be a page in their book. They are exciting, contemporary and devilishly clever. Their relationship is tempestuous and challenging but if it prevails, isn't that the test of longevity? I am convinced that they are the perfect couple and life partners in the true sense of the word. Will they grow old together? Who knows? I'm betting that they will at least grow fat together. Now, that's food for thought.

MY FRIEND, THE SERIAL KILLER

I was having a few drinks with a mate, some time back. He's a bit of a social challenge and certainly not your typical alpha male: fixed rate mortgage, two point five children, dogs, cat and a budgie. Unfortunately, it was all getting a bit too much for him and also a bit boring, so, he told his wife that he was a serial killer. She didn't seem to mind. As long as he wasn't having it off with another woman, things could be worked out.

Although we were never close, I immediately warmed to this lady and thought that this was the kind of wife that a man needs — somebody who will support you through thick and thin (as long as you're not having it off with another woman). The truth of the matter is that I am more likely to be a mass murderer than he is but one tends to let insecure people run with their fantasies. I didn't like to sound too interested so I changed the subject to sporting matters, which is far more appropriate when you are socializing at Hooters.

In truth, I think the reason for this mid-life crisis was our mutual friend, Basil. Bazza had shacked up with this real estate chick and they were living the high life without any responsibility. You know how it is. You're knee deep in kiddy poop and your buddy is high fiving with Beyoncé and the beautiful people. I wish I could have provided more support but I was pissed-off with Basil myself. He was my guest when he calmly walked up to the official table and ate the first prize at the Somerville Apple and Pear Festival. What a worm!

I don't often wax lyrical about the integrity of life but two point five children is a commendable contribution to colonization. I can also understand that constant rebellion is good enough reason to chop one in half but where are we going from here? The young people are living in a different world. They have tatts on their tush, rings through their nipples and you would love to shove that cell phone up their ass. Thank God that I am a cool customer and a friend of their father. Respect has always been a sacred word in our family.

I don't know where the pail of horseshit came from. I didn't see it coming. Obviously, one tends to relax after a skin-full of the amber fluid and we may have been less than vigilant. I believe that there was a commitment to return in time for supper and this deadline appears to have well passed. No wonder she wasn't fussed by a serial killer. The lady was a psychopath in her own right and I could only feel sorry for the horse. It's not every day that someone beats the crap out of you.

Domestic violence is something that has always worried me and I felt very nervous about being on the perimeter of this little shindig. Needless to say, I was shocked to learn that I was being blamed for the whole episode, from both sides. Don't you just hate it when somebody turns on you like that? I was best man at his wedding and even used to baby sit those snotty-nosed kids when the parents needed a break. I always covered for him, when the need arose.

If I can get his story straight, he was having a cup of tea with two nuns that he knew when I arrived and dragged him off to Hooters. I think that she was prepared to believe this far-fetched story because it gave her a good excuse to demand the termination of our relationship. What! Me a bad influence.

My friend, the serial killer, actually has a name but it tends to embarrass him and so I often refrain from spreading the word. Not anymore! His name is Haddock. Don't ask me how or why. We just call him Fish.

The early days!

Fish was in my class at school and we used to sit together. We shared our homework and just about everything else, including mutually amorous intentions towards the younger sister of one of our class-mates. Of course, the odds of ever being alone with her were monumental. Not only were we were both boarders but the attitude of the Jesuits was inexplicable. They just did not did not encourage liaisons with the opposite sex. In fact, it is said that they even refuse to condone people having sex, while standing up. It might lead to dancing. The only outlet for our pent-up frustrations was the sporting arena and we both excelled at football, both forms of pool and table tennis. Our big social release was the Saturday night movie.

The only programming blemish was the inclination of our teachers to continually revisit any film that touched on the subject of higher learning. *Tom Brown's Schooldays* was given a real pasting and when I finally departed into the world of long trousers and paisley ties, I had seen *Goodbye Mr Chips* six times. This was a period piece of an era that I was unfamiliar with but, nevertheless, I was impressed by the respect that the pupils bestowed on this kind and gracious teacher. I might add that he was in no way related to Ronald McDonald.

Fish was an out of town boy and the family residence was extremely rural. The corn was as high as an elephant's eye and there were all manner of animals that appeared to be out of control. However, they never strayed far from the farm house. His mother must have blessed the arrival of their first television set. This phenomenon had been recently introduced into the country and it had an immediate impact in isolated areas. It slowed down the birth rate.

I was often invited to the farm for part of the term holidays and this was a noble gesture because there were already eight mouths to feed and my appetite was voracious. I also managed to fall off their horses, break their farm machinery and embarrass Fish by being a total city slicker. I like to think that I earned my keep by providing good advice to his two younger brothers (Halibut and Herring) on how to pick up girls. With some pride, I have recently learned that each of them has been married three times.

In my youth, guys were not generally that confident so this gave us brash people a head start. We kidded, cajoled and canoodled our way around the book club, the netball team and the YWCA. For our trouble, we were branded as being totally promiscuous. I had no idea what this meant but wore the mantle proudly.

Although my influence was ever-present, Fish eventually pulled back a little to concentrate on studies, career opportunities and girls with something between their ears. Very admirable, I thought and he would probably benefit in the long run. As long as he didn't forget his old mate.

The best years of your life!

I didn't make it to university. He did and performed with honor and distinction. What more can you ask than that? His parents were very proud of him, even though it meant an overseas posting for post graduate work. This was where Haddock met his hippy girl friend. She was a fellow student and spent most of the day dissecting confused animals in a laboratory sponsored by the Cancer Institute of America. At least that's what he thought CIA stood for.

You may remember Sadaam Hussein's recently deceased cousin, often referred to as Chemical Ali. My friend's favorite squeeze was called Nadia Nitrate by everyone who knew her and there was some Slavic background in there somewhere because she had an explosive temper. Fish was in a bit of a stew because these were difficult times and the Russians were not our friends. The Cold War was warming up and Nadia had a poster of Ché Guevara above her bed. This was not an uncommon situation on campus but she was working for the CIA. Did anybody smell a rat?

Evidently, there were more rats in the laboratory than people first thought and a whole sleeper cell was exposed, Nadia amongst them. Naturally, all her friends were subjected to intense scrutiny and Fish was lucky to get out with his reputation intact. He returned to Australia with his tail between his legs and I could tell that he had been damaged by the whole experience. I felt that the best way to get him back on track was to get somebody else's tail between his legs, so I introduced him to Molly.

Molly liked Haddock and this was not so surprising. He was male and breathing. Co-incidentally, some of her ancestors were fishmongers in the old country. Her great grandfather was a barrow boy and his daughter, young Molly Malone, was a well-know figure around the Dublin markets during the tough times and she was quite outrageous. In order to make ends meet, the young lady resorted to nocturnal activities that were definitely frowned upon. In Grafton St they called her the trollop with the scallops.

After the virago from Vladivostok, Fish was ready for somebody like Molly who was great fun and her musical tastes were similar to his own. She liked Enya, Mary Black and anybody called Paddy. His manners were impeccable; he was attentive and always the diplomat. What can you say about a man who always remembers your birthday but not your age? Like me, he was a charming, urbane, sensitive, tolerant and caring individual. However, I think that he could have burrowed into my cave of virtues a little further. Whereas I was a fine conversationalist, an excellent sportsman, humorously attuned and artistically aware, he was decidedly dull.

You can understand that the relationship was doomed from the start. Molly liked the sex but she wasn't a one guy gal and he was a little inexperienced. The Fish man was not only wet behind the ears but also slow on the uptake. Why did he never question all those male cousins and uncles that she kept producing? Nobody has a family that large. Eventually, the unthinkable occurred. Molly was doing Christmas relief work in the toy department of a city department store when she was discovered *in flagrante delicto* with Santa Claus during his coffee break. Relief work, indeed!

I suppose people will say that I am to blame for introducing him to someone like Molly but I can live with that. In the end, I think that he was happy to be out of it. He actually confided to me that he didn't really like Van Morrison, Bono or Irish stew. There you go. Keeping up appearances! Fortunately, he maintained his craving for the Guinness brew and this helped sustain us both over the ensuing months. In fact, we had three glorious years boozing, belching and bonking our way around the Melbourne party scene before he succumbed once again to the tender trap. This time it was terminal.

> *Some starry night, when her kisses make you tingle*
> *she'll hold you tight and you'll hate yourself for being single.*

I think it was Sammy Cahn who penned these ridiculous lyrics for Frank Sinatra. Talk about pressure. On top of that, it was a leap year and Mauve was no shrinking violet. She had convinced Fish that being a bachelor was no life for a single man. An Easter wedding was proposed and he was deliberating on this prospect over a few sloe gins at a discreet topless bar that I had recently discovered. I thought that this would be an ideal venue for a good heart to heart. If destabilization could be achieved, it would be here.

You wouldn't believe it. He spent ten minutes gaping into his firewater and then came out with the astounding statement: *I'm getting married. At Easter!* Of course, I thought that he was off his rocker. After all, who comes into a topless bar and spends the time staring into their drink. I used all my renowned persuasive skills to provide sound reasons why he should think a bit more about this life-changing decision but he was intransient. I even introduced him to Candy, Mandy, Randy and Frank but he would not be moved. Was I losing my touch? Who was it who said: *No matter how much you push the envelope, it'll still be stationery?*

So, an Easter wedding it was and I scrubbed up pretty well as the best man. The bridal party was dressed in purple and the guests dined on caviar, lobster and smoked salmon. Halibut and Herring had grown into strapping young lads and I could see that my tuition was bearing fruit. They both had serious crumpet in tow and things were looking rosy for everyone. It's a bit surprising that Mauve and I didn't become close because we both liked horses. She was keen to ride them and I bet on them. Of course, I didn't need much space to accommodate my obsession. Just some elbow room at the tote window. She needed a few acres of pasture for Mozart and Tchaikovsky, her two equestrian ponies. This meant that the couple had to live out of town a bit and this suited her because it would mean that Haddock could distance himself from me. The strategy must have worked because all of a sudden Fish was the father of two and President of the local Lions club. My first visit ended in disaster.

I had over-indulged over dinner but she wouldn't let me stay the night. So I drove home under dark skies on an almost deserted road. In the distance I saw this very small car heading towards me. It was so small that I deduced that there were probably Leprechauns aboard. The vehicle started getting bigger and I wondered why. Then it hit me. I was driving on the wrong side of the road. The paramedics said that I was lucky to be alive and my lawyer confessed that I was lucky not to be in jail. All up, the repatriation took about five months but I did receive a get well card from Fish, Mauve, the two kiddies plus Mozart and Tchaikovsky. He then sent another to advise that he was to become a father again. Evidently, because I departed early, they decided to have sex.

It's hard to know when Fish became bored with the whole deal. However, he was excited when I advised him that Hooters were building their first down-under franchise only a few miles from their retreat. That's why I am disappointed with that nun story that he trotted out. My own sister was a nun and I know for a fact that they needed more than tea to help them through their monastic duties.

I don't know where my friend goes from here. His academic brilliance will surely be passed on to young Mackerel and the others but I am worried about the psychological damage that may be caused by the breakdown in his personal relationship. She who must be obeyed is all powerful and I can understand his desire to break the shackles. She is the kind of person who will admit that she may not always be right but she is never wrong.

Nevertheless, boredom is one thing but it is a quantum leap from lapdog to serial killer. Perhaps there are too many dogs in the relationship. Can he reclaim the domestic harmony that he enjoyed before Bach, Offenbach and De Pussy came along (her household pets)? And where do I fit into the scheme of things? I am not a favorite son and never will be but why would you look elsewhere for a marriage guidance councilor? I have seen it all so many times and people say that I throw the best divorce parties. Perhaps I'll set up shop. I believe that there is a vacant office going in the Hooters building.

WORKING FOR THE MAN

The bean counter

Honky Tonk Man

Blood, sweat and tears

I've been a working man all my life. My local baker put it ever so succinctly when he paraphrased the lyrics of that evergreen song that was first penned in the forties: *You lift sixteen buns and what do you get; another day older and deeper in debt?* At least he was in business for himself. The heroes of my final stories were all subservient to their paymasters but that is not to intimate that they didn't enjoy their work because they did.

As I do. I like to think that these few moments that we have had together will be a satisfactory experience for us both. I am sure that your pants are now in superior condition and if you are female, I hope that nothing that I may have said will get your knickers in a knot. It's not easy being a politically incorrect person.

THE BEAN COUNTER

It has taken me quite some time to come to terms with the fact that I am not infallible. Brash and over-confident! I was all of that but I should have been more respectful of the government agency that finally brought us down. In the end, I got off pretty lightly. I should be dead. I used to be Al Capone's tax accountant.

Al was a pretty confident type of person himself. With good reason! He could have been arraigned on any of the two hundred murders that he committed before his twenty-first birthday. In fact, some people wondered why there were so many candles on his birthday cake. That he was finally indicted on income tax evasion was eleven years of bad luck for Al and a lifetime of apprehension for me. I had also felt personally slighted, as I believe that some people thought I should have spent more time with the Income Tax Act, rather than the booze and broads at The Cotton Club. What can I say? I was young and insatiable and this kind of lifestyle was a heady mix for a young lad from the boondocks.

Those innocent years were a lifetime away from the powerful temptations that came with prohibition and easy money. Perhaps this is why it was such an enticement. We didn't have any money and I don't know how my pop managed to provide for such a large family. I also don't know why we had such a large family. My younger sister explained that our breadwinner was a sex maniac. I didn't know what a sex maniac was and it was a measure of my slow learning capacities that she knew about these things before I did.

Our mother was as optimistic as one could be under the circumstances and always maintained that we shouldn't worry. Everything was in God's hands. Not for long. I have to admit to being a bit of a rogue and the siphoning of the Sabbath collection was one of my specialties. Lesser mortals would have splurged such a windfall on superfluous excess but not me. I learnt to manage money responsibly. A brace of rabbits always appeared in our kitchen, a few hours before our main Sunday meal and Ma always used to thank God for these provisions. If only she had known the truth?

In this world there are professionally trained experts and those who have graduated through the school of hard knocks. You wouldn't want to visit my alma mater. They say that necessity is the mother of invention and I don't doubt that. If young Mr Invention had siblings, they would be called Stealing, Coercion, Cruelty and various other street crimes. Once having accumulated the necessary funds, the challenge is to perpetuate your income without having to explain from whence it came.

At first, this was easy. You owned a machine gun and nobody asked questions. Then this person called the Taxation Commissioner came along and life became difficult. I think that it is fair to say that many of my confreres were unfamiliar with the concept of taxation and you can understand that they needed advice. Patiently, I explained that bumping off the guy would not be productive as he would be replaced by somebody else. I soon became creative and created false identities and occupations for any number of gangsters in the Chicago area. You know how it is. You do good work and you get yourself a reputation.

I didn't know Capone during his switchblade years, when he acquired the Scarface tag: a little nick, after an altercation over a babe. Wouldn't you know it? When he moved to Chicago from New York, I was counting the cards in one of Bugsy Moran's speakeasies. On most nights I was a little intoxicated. Make that a lot intoxicated. When Al offered me a job, I thought he wanted an Axe Advisor and, given his reputation, I thought it an ideal position to be able to wipe out all my creditors in one foul swoop. So, I accepted.

In the light of sober reflection, I realized that the numbers didn't stack up. He was making good money for a furniture salesman but his outgoings for bribery and intimidation of public officials were astronomical. I came to the conclusion that it was pointless submitting a tax return if these kinds of payments were not acceptable deductions. It was a critical misjudgment. Some guy called Eliot Ness discovered that we hadn't filed a tax return for two years and the process servers started salivating. I told them that I, personally, hadn't filed for ten years. They didn't seem to care.

Obviously, this crime fighter had a bee in his bonnet over Capone and I didn't know why. Most of the other guys at City Hall were happy with their Christmas bonuses, which we paid without fail every March and August. Unfortunately, there was a hard core who were untouchable and they made life complicated. It was enough to drive you to drink except that Ness was there before you. He closed down most of our breweries and Al was convinced that he was working for the Rechabites.

As if the law wasn't a big enough distraction, Capone's arch enemy, Bugs Moran, was even more intrusive. Assassination attempts were made on both Al and his chief terminator, Jack McGurn. The man was forced to ride around in a bullet-proof Cadillac. You can imagine what that did to petrol consumption. Nevertheless, through it all, income flowed into the coffers at the rate of one hundred million dollars per year and I was busy supervising gambling, bootlegging and prostitution. Fortunately, Al used to help out. I think he personally interviewed every hooker we hired.

It wasn't easy living in the shadow of eternal damnation, although these aren't my words. Whenever I delivered the monthly order of altar wine to the cathedral, they gave me a preferential pew outside the confessional. It was always a tough two hours and I must admit that I sometimes did harbor feelings of regret and remorse but only for a moment. I often quote those immortal words of Oscar Wilde: *It is better to repent a sin than regret the loss of a pleasure.*

Al Capone ended up with syphilis but I never did. I am grateful for small mercies. He was rather bald from an early age so you wonder how he became so much of a ladies' man. I suppose that you would have to admit that he did have a strong personality and I can see how that might be appealing to some. My own personality was somewhat tarnished by alcohol and, with the constant stress of pressure from without and within, the workplace environment became riddled with rancor and recklessness. We made mistakes but that's life. You're riding high in April, shot down in May.

I suppose it is easy to dwell on the bad times. You tend to forget what a character he was and generous to a fault. During the holiday season, Al always had a few headliners over to entertain the boys, who were often holed up somewhere: and I don't have to tell you how he felt about St Valentine's Day. What a romantic. What a massacre. The pundits still rate it the gangland killing of the century and Al was always grateful to Machine Gun McGurn. It was the event that catapulted this erstwhile racketeer to Public Enemy No.1.

©davorr-Fotolia.com

Al's boys: Good help is hard to find.

I must say that I was always a little nervous of McGurn. He had orchestrated the massacre and was a bad man in his own right. Joe E. Lewis, the comedian and former singer had learnt that to his detriment. He had his vocal chords cut because he chose to move on from the mobster's night-club. The guy used to sing like Frank Sinatra. Of course, nobody could sing like the stool pigeons at Al's trial. They had copies of all my most intimate misappropriations and they were quoting taxation projections that would even give a treasury official an orgasm. Naturally, I was deflated, even though I wasn't their target. However, I was singled out for a number of misdemeanors. Evidently, they couldn't find a compliance statement for Murder Incorporated, which was one of our conglomerates that specialized in asset transfers.

When they escorted Al off to Alcatraz, I became redundant. I also became scarce. You do your best but sometimes that's not good enough. At least, I missed the ignominy of the slammer. Prisoner AZ-85 didn't. In the early days, his influence was profound and his internment was relatively comfortable with mood lighting, an antique writing desk and selected French wines on tap. An uncompromising warden soon changed all that and he was subject to the most humiliating indignities. He was even stabbed in the back by a fellow inmate. Can you believe that? Then, racially abused. When he was transferred to the prison bathhouse, they called him the wop with a mop.

The sad thing for me was the loss of face amongst my peers — not that I was qualified, mind you. Then they repealed prohibition. I was left with two thousand liters of under proof whisky, which I thought might get me the kind of liquid funds that I was looking for. The firewater was found to be 97% acid wash but it sold reasonably well as rust remover.

Al Capone is long gone and so is Alcatraz. It is now a tourist attraction. My type of creative accounting is still in vogue but the belching bodyguards have been replaced by personal assistants in tight skirts. Life moves on. If you are a person with taxation expertise, I do hope that you use it for good rather than evil. We will all sleep better if we know that the bean counters are on the side of the angels.

Sadly, I don't believe that the angels will be scrutinizing my credentials any time soon. At the top of this heart-rending reminiscence, I was grateful for the gift of life but that is all behind me now. I look forward to renewing acquaintances with old friends and I am sure that a hot time will be had by all. Perhaps even Al and Bugs have been able to patch up their differences. I hope so. After all, we are a long time dead.

HONKY TONK MAN

I like to make people happy, even if only for a short period of time. Throughout my life I have been a team player and one who is always glad to embrace new trends but, at the same time, preserve acceptable standards. The music business has always been tough and uncompromising and I like to think that I have been a survivor — in fact, one of the great survivors. I knocked back the gig as the saloon pianist on the Titanic. Fortunately, I was on the wrong side of the Atlantic at the time.

Piano players were a dime a dozen in New York City during the turn of the century. I had lobbed in from southern parts and tried to team up with some established groups but to no avail. If you were on your own, you either played in a church or a brothel. If you were really good, you might end up in a music hall and that's what happened to me. I shared the load with a character called Scott Joplin, who was experimenting with a new form of music called Ragtime. I could see where he was coming from. You really do get sick of playing the same old melody time and time again.

I can remember tickling the ivories at some R and R lounges during the last war. The hotel didn't pay you so you charged ten bucks to rattle off a song. Any song. Well, almost any song. "White Christmas" was one hundred dollars and "In the Mood" was three hundred dollars. You hoped that such a price tag might put them off but usually it didn't.

Of course, there were places where the rustle of money wasn't tolerated and that meant that I had a pay-check. One of my favorites was the Algonquin Hotel and it was great fun to mess around with Dorothy Parker and the Round Table group. This was the lady who proclaimed that it was just like her to put all her eggs in the one bastard.

Louis Armstrong had come down from Chicago and was playing with Fletcher Henderson: and there was no one who was bigger than Bessie Smith. She was six feet tall and weighed in at over two hundred pounds. If you happened to be just a little off-key, you would get this withering stare and believe me, you paid attention from that moment on. I liked the buzz of the twenties and it was good for musicians. We used to get free booze at the speakeasies and the dames were incredible. At times, I was a bit apprehensive because some of those goons could be a bit trigger-happy when they imbibed in too much of the sauce. Nevertheless, my kind of entertainment was relatively safe compared to others. Both Abraham Lincoln and John Dillinger were killed because they went to the theater.

I must admit that there has been criticism of certain practices in our profession. Some people believe that pianists aren't patriotic because they don't stand up for the national anthem. I had almost convinced them that the average keyboard player needs to be close to his keys when that idiot Jerry Lee Lewis started prancing around in front of his upright in a totally vertical position. If I were to take a stand, I would have to say that I am as patriotic as the next person and I think my work with John McCormack bears that out.

His version of *The Battle Hymn of the Republic* has no equal and who can forget our appearance at Carnegie Hall to a standing ovation from the cream of New Yorker society and visiting dignitaries from far and wide. I have to say that I was a pretty versatile kind of guy and was equally at home at Madison Square Garden. What an earner that could be. During the Gene Tunney and Jack Dempsey world title fight in Philadelphia in 1926, I was playing advertising jingles in between the rounds. The contest only lasted ten rounds and spelt the end for the Manassa Mauler. There were over 120,000 fans in attendance and many of them remarked on the clarity of my pianoforte.

I am not a keen sports fan although I do like non-combative contests like pool and billiards. I can still remember that ten ball, cue ball, winner take all challenge in Queens when Minnesota Fats was at his top. His opponent was the Australian star Walter Lindrum and it took twenty minutes to clear the air of cigar smoke before they announced the decision. The Aussies went wild and I stoked up an improvised version of their unofficial national anthem, Waltzing Matilda. These are strange lyrics — something about a vagabond jive bunny who dives into a pond to evade the constabulary. It reminded me of Sinatra at Lake Tahoe when the gambling authorities came after him.

I would have liked to play with Frank but never did. He moved in exalted circles and the bobby-soxers thought that he was cool — even hip. I'm afraid that I was a bit square but his overwhelming popularity gave me the incentive to expand my interests. I really had to. During the depression, my kind of music lost popularity to the country folk, who could sing a dirge like nobody could. The blue yodeler, Jimmy Rogers, traversed the country by freight train and sang of misery and despair. On top of that, the guitar became the musical instrument of choice. It was far more portable than a baby grand and you could use it as a pillow, if the need arose.

I met one of these guitar guys a little later down the track. Elvis Presley was a truck driver and I thought that he could be good for me. During elections, they used to mount a piano on a flat bed truck and drive it around the town. That seemed a good idea to me and we collaborated on a few projects but they came to nothing. Not that there weren't some good ideas floated around. My two songs *Tan Leather Shoes* and *Bake House Rock* were promising but Elvis was hauled off to jail over a misdemeanor and we lost contact.

When the standards came back into vogue, I had just about done my dash. Moon River was topping the charts and I was holed up with a washed up alcoholic singer on a river boat in Illinois. You can be really brought back to earth, can't you? The dame had been involved in some brouhaha down south and all she wanted to do was forget. So, when in doubt, shack up with the piano player.

The broad looked a lot like Ava Gardner and this is probably why I found her so appealing, along with the fact that she only drank beer. I like a cheap date. Unfortunately, because she consumed so much of the amber fluid, my economic perspective became totally flawed.

I have dated quite a few singers. I mean, how easy was it? In those days, you didn't need eHarmony to get to first base — just some convincing patter and those heavily insured digits of mine. When you are down amongst the ebony and ivory, you are always in close proximity to the intimate nearness of a slinky cabaret dress and I was usually the only one wearing underclothes. The wash of cheap perfume engulfs you like a tsunami of temptation and you will succumb with hardly a suggestion of prevarication.

When you are getting on a bit, you can only take this life for so long. You crave good company and some of these gamblers and carpetbaggers were indolent pigs. I had been working for wages most of my life and didn't have a lot to show for it. All the same, you don't mind if someone appreciates you for what you are and what you do. Today, I am the musical supervisor at an old people's home. I can relive past memories with the other in-mates and we do it regularly — not that I am the only musician in residence. There are a number of rock 'n roll veterans around but personally, I believe they are just here for the drugs.

BLOOD, SWEAT AND TEARS

I have known adulation, adoration and rapturous ovations. I am widely traveled and have enjoyed stimulating destinations such as London, New York, Milan, Madrid, Barcelona and Buenos Aires. I am the envy of my peers and the larrikin of La Scala. Until recently, I was Pavarotti's handkerchief.

My childhood was quite unspectacular. I was a bit highly strung so you can imagine why I moved into the business that I did. Certainly, my forebears weren't in the entertainment industry. They were definitely working class but made a name for themselves in the great flu pandemic of 1918. These were tough times and disease was rampant. Linen was in great demand and soon everybody was clamoring for hankies. Every bedroom drawer had handkerchiefs lying on top of each other. No wonder they proliferated so much. In no time at all, I had an extended family and they were very ambitious.

It was my grandmother who first made it into the silk department: a Bologna department store, I believe. Kith and kin were impressed and there was a lot of support and encouragement from her cousins, the Serviettes. They had infiltrated the stately homes of Italy and were rather pompous. Nevertheless, there were also a few plebs in the family: very colorful table accessories that serviced the restaurants, bistros and cafés in the lower end of town. Some of them were even red and white. A lot of people aren't aware that handkerchiefs have their own brand of racial discrimination but the fact is that if you're not white you're not kosher. There is always a push for change from contemporary activists but in my world, conservatism reigns supreme. Even that great musical genius Louis Armstrong opted for a white handkerchief.

I was plucked from obscurity at an early age but there was not too much disharmony because two of my siblings went with me. It was sale time in Modena and Pav got three handkerchiefs for a tenor. Initially there were no favorites and we were continually rotated. It was rather dark and dingy down there at the ass end of his pocket but I eventually graduated to his waist-coat and, finally, I ended up his sleeve. All power to me. One of my relatives was indentured to David Copperfield and he didn't know whether he was Arthur or Martha.

You wouldn't believe it but my very first appearance on stage was at Carnegie Hall. The great man had a cold and he didn't want to sneeze all over the orchestra. He would do much worse to them later in life but let's not go into that. At rehearsals, Joan Sutherland had delivered her now famous retort: *You are fat, Luciano. I am big.* I thought we must have been on the Jerry Springer set but there were no tears and I was not required. They were great friends.

I didn't always appear. He did Pagliacci, Rigoletto and Tosca without me but I was back on deck for the World Cup performance and any number of concert presentations that were held in parks, gardens and football stadiums. Our boy was pretty keen on the soccer and he also had a fascination with horses. I have a nephew in Australia who has a mentor who is similarly fascinated. Nevertheless, if you are a handkerchief, you don't want to spend too much time around horses. They are rather dirty animals and yet they feel that they have no need of a clean-up. It was no surprise to me that my old gran went silk.

You may have seen a number of cowboy flicks where the bad guys had to wave a white flag as a form of surrender. Let me say, right now, that these flags are not in any way related to my pure form of showbiz. Pavarotti waved me on many occasions to his adoring fans and I can admit to being a little giddy at times. All the same, applause always sustains a true thespian and I often relive these glorious moments. I don't think that I worked any harder than in his concert at Barbados in 1997. I can tell you that it was hot and we were outside. He was dripping sweat like a movie critic at a Tarantino preview.

His passing was a sad day for us all and my whole family was working overtime on the morning of the funeral. The whole country was crying. I know that this was not a good time to be thinking of oneself but I couldn't help but wonder what was going to become of me. Nicoletta Mantovani, the widow, was rather ambivalent as far as I was concerned and had me shipped off to the Chinese laundry and then promptly forgot about me. That's right. They forgot about me. I'm still here.

It's not a bad life and Ah Choo treats me well. I am now probably too old for all that traveling and the pension is quite adequate. I am never out of pocket and have become quite a fashion plate whenever I am pressed into service. Of course, tea with the Tong is not quite the same as pasta with Pavarotti and I do think that these people are a little too aggressive. When I am not appreciated, I take great delight in throwing their old proverbs back at them: *Man who sneezes without hanky takes matters into his own hands.*

Gerry Burke

Melbourne, Australia

ABOUT THE AUTHOR!

This is Gerry Burke's second book. Gerry was educated at Xavier College and subsequently joined the workforce as an accountant, spending some of his time in New Guinea. He later changed direction and became a copywriter and Creative Director with a number of international advertising agencies.

Along the way he operated his own boutique agency and production company and provided comedy scripts for local entertainers.

It will surprise no-one to learn that he is seriously involved in the thoroughbred industry and has raced seventeen horses and still counting.

He remains a committed bachelor and lives in Melbourne.

Also available by Gerry Burke and published by IUniverse:
From Beer to Paternity
- One man's journey through life as we know it

Printed in the United States
By Bookmasters